WHAT TURNS ON
A KRYPTONIAN?

Superman is an alien . . . an extraterrestrial. His humanoid frame is doubtless the result of parallel evolution.

A specific niche in the ecology calls for a certain shape, a certain size, certain capabilities, certain eating habits.

Be not deceived by appearances.

Superman is no relative to homo sapiens.

What arouses his mating urge? Did Kryptonian women carry some subtle mating cue at appropriate times of the year?

Whatever it is, Lois Lane probably doesn't have it!

—From: "Man of Steel
Woman of Kleenex"

Also by Larry Niven
Published by Ballantine Books:

CONVERGENT SERIES

THE FLIGHT OF THE HORSE

A GIFT FROM EARTH

A HOLE IN SPACE

THE LONG ARM OF GIL HAMILTON

NEUTRON STAR

PROTECTOR

RINGWORLD

TALES OF KNOWN SPACE:
  The Universe of Larry Niven

WORLD OF PTAVVS

A WORLD OUT OF TIME

THE FLYING SORCERERS
  (with David Gerrold)

All The Myriad Ways

LARRY NIVEN

A Del Rey Book

BALLANTINE BOOKS • NEW YORK

A Del Rey Book
Published by Ballantine Books

ACKNOWLEDGMENTS:

"Unfinished Story #1," Copyright 1970, Mercury Press, Inc.

"Not Long Before the End," Copyright 1969, Mercury Press,
Inc.

"All the Myriad Ways," Copyright 1968, Galaxy Publishing
Corp.

"Theory and Practice of Teleportation," Copyright 1969, Galaxy
Publishing Corp.

"The Jigsaw Man," first appeared in DANGEROUS VISIONS,
ed. by Harlan Ellison, Copyright 1967 by Harlan Ellison

"Becalmed in Hell," Copyright 1965, Mercury Press, Inc.

"For a Foggy Night," Copyright 1971, Mercury Press, Inc.

ISBN 0-345-28196-9

Manufactured in the United States of America

First Edition: June 1971
Fourth Printing: November 1978

Cover art by Dean Ellis

to MARILYN alias Fuzzy Pink
who starred in a couple of stories
and inspired others

CONTENTS

ALL THE MYRIAD WAYS   1

PASSERBY   12

FOR A FOGGY NIGHT   28

WAIT IT OUT   36

THE JIGSAW MAN   45

NOT LONG BEFORE THE END   59

UNFINISHED STORY #1   72

UNFINISHED STORY #2   73

MAN OF STEEL
    WOMAN OF KLEENEX   74

EXERCISE IN SPECULATION: *THE
    THEORY AND PRACTICE
    OF TELEPORTATION*   83

THE THEORY AND PRACTICE OF
    TIME TRAVEL   110

INCONSTANT MOON   124

WHAT CAN YOU SAY ABOUT
    CHOCOLATE COVERED
    MANHOLE COVERS?   154

BECALMED IN HELL   167

ALL THE
MYRIAD WAYS

ALL THE MYRIAD WAYS

There were timelines branching and branching, a megauniverse of universes, millions more every minute. Billions? Trillions? Trimble didn't understand the theory, though God knows he'd tried. The universe split every time someone made a decision. Split, so that every decision ever made could go both ways. Every choice made by every man, woman and child on Earth was reversed in the universe next door. It was enough to confuse any citizen, let alone Detective-Lieutenant Gene Trimble, who had other problems.

Senseless suicides, senseless crimes. A city-wide epidemic. It had hit other cities too. Trimble suspected that it was world wide, that other nations were simply keeping it quiet.

Trimble's sad eyes focussed on the clock. Quitting time. He stood up to go home, and slowly sat down again. For he had his teeth in the problem, and he couldn't let go.

Not that he was really accomplishing anything.

But if he left now, he'd only have to take it up again tomorrow.

Go, or stay?

And the branchings began again. Gene Trimble thought of other universes parallel to this one, and a parallel Gene Trimble in each one. Some had left early. Many had left on time, and were now halfway home to dinner, out to a movie, watching a strip show, racing to the scene of another death. Streaming out of police headquarters in all their multitudes, leaving a multitude

1

of Trimbles behind them. Each of these trying to deal, alone, with the city's endless, inexplicable parade of suicides.

Gene Trimble spread the morning paper on his desk. From the bottom drawer he took his gun-cleaning equipment, then his .45. He began to take the gun apart.

The gun was old but serviceable. He'd never fired it except on the target range, and never expected to. To Trimble, cleaning his gun was like knitting, a way to keep his hands busy while his mind wandered off. Turn the screws, don't lose them. Lay the parts out in order.

Through the closed door to his office came the sounds of men hurrying. Another emergency? The department couldn't handle it all. Too many suicides, too many casual murders, not enough men.

Gun oil. Oiled rag. Wipe each part. Put it back in place.

Why would a man like Ambrose Harmon go off a building?

In the early morning light he lay, more a stain than a man, thirty-six stories below the edge of his own penthouse roof. The pavement was splattered red for yards around him. The stains were still wet. Harmon had landed on his face. He wore a bright silk dressing gown and a sleeping jacket with a sash.

Others would take samples of his blood, to learn if he had acted under the influence of alcohol or drugs. There was little to be learned from seeing him in his present condition.

"But why was he up so early?" Trimble wondered. For the call had come in at 8:03, just as Trimble arrived at headquarters.

"So late, you mean." Bentley had beaten him to the scene by twenty minutes. "We called some of his friends. He was at an all-night poker game. Broke up around six o'clock."

"Did Harmon lose?"

"Nope. He won almost five hundred bucks."

"That fits," Trimble said in disgust. "No suicide note?"

"Maybe they've found one. Shall we go up and see?"

"We won't find a note," Trimble predicted.

Even three months earlier Trimble would have thought, *How incredible!* or, *Who could have pushed him?* Now, riding up in the elevator, he thought only, *Reporters.* For Ambrose Harmon was news. Even among this past year's epidemic of suicides, Ambrose Harmon's death would stand out like Lyndon Johnson in a lineup.

He was a prominent member of the community, a man of dead and wealthy grandparents. Perhaps the huge inheritance, four years ago, had gone to his head. He had invested tremendous sums to back hairbrained, quixotic causes.

Now, because one of the hairbrained causes had paid off, he was richer than ever. The Crosstime Corporation already held a score of patents on inventions imported from alternate time tracks. Already those inventions had started more than one industrial revolution. And Harmon was the money behind Crosstime. He would have been the world's next billionaire —had he not walked off his balcony.

They found a roomy, luxuriously furnished apartment in good order, and a bed turned down for the night. The only sign of disorder was the clothing— slacks, sweater, a silk turtleneck shirt, knee-length shoesocks, no underwear—piled on a chair in the bedroom. The toothbrush had been used.

He got ready for bed, Trimble thought. He brushed his teeth, and then he went out to look at the sunrise. A man who kept late hours like that, he wouldn't see the sunrise very often. He watched the sunrise, and when it was over, he jumped.

Why?

They were all like that. Easy, spontaneous decisions. The victim/killers walked off bridges or stepped from their balconies or suddenly flung themselves in front of subway trains. They strolled halfway across a freeway, or swallowed a full bottle of laudanum. None of the methods showed previous planning. Whatever was used, the victim had had it all along; he never actually went out and *bought* a suicide weapon. The victim rarely dressed for the occasion, or used makeup, as an ordinary suicide would. Usually there was no note.

Harmon fit the pattern perfectly.

"Like Richard Corey," said Bentley.

"Who?"

"Richard Corey, the man who had everything. 'And Richard Corey, one calm summer night, went home and put a bullet through his head.' You know what I think?"

"If you've got an idea, let's have it."

"The suicides all started about a month after Crosstime got started. I think one of the Crosstime ships brought back a new bug from some alternate timeline."

"A suicide bug?"

Bentley nodded.

"You're out of your mind."

"I don't think so. Gene, do you know how many Crosstime pilots have killed themselves in the last year? More than twenty percent!"

"Oh?"

"Look at the records. Crosstime has about twenty vehicles in action now, but in the past year they've employed sixty-two pilots. Three disappeared. Fifteen are dead, and all but two died by suicide."

"I didn't know that." Trimble was shaken.

"It was bound to happen sometime. Look at the alternate worlds they've found so far. The Nazi world. The Red Chinese world, half bombed to death. The ones that are so totally bombed, that Crosstime can't even find out who did it. The one with the Black Plague mutation, and no penicillin until Crosstime came along. Sooner or later—"

"Maybe, maybe. I don't buy your bug, though. If the suicides are a new kind of plague, what about the other crimes?"

"Same bug."

"Uh uh. But I think we'll check up on Crosstime."

Trimble's hands finished with the gun and laid it on the desk. He was hardly aware of it. Somewhere in the back of his mind was a prodding sensation: the *handle*, the piece he needed to solve the puzzle.

He's spent most of the day studying Crosstime, Inc. News stories, official handouts, personal interviews. The incredible suicide rate among Crosstime pilots could not be coincidence. He wondered why nobody had noticed it before.

It was slow going. With Crosstime travel, as with relativity, you had to throw away reason and use only logic. Trimble had sweated it out. Even the day's murders had not distracted him.

They were typical, of a piece with the preceding eight months' crime wave. A man had shot his foreman with a gun bought an hour earlier, then strolled off toward police headquarters. A woman had moved through the back row of a dark theater, using an ice pick to stab members of the audience through the backs of their seats. She had chosen only young men. They had killed without heat, without concealment; they had surrendered without fear or bravado. Perhaps it was another kind of suicide.

Time for coffee, Trimble thought, responding unconsciously to dry throat plus a muzziness in the mouth plus slight fatigue. He set his hands to stand up, and—

The image came to him of an endless row of Trimbles, lined up like the repeated images in facing mirrors. But each image was slightly different. He would go get the coffee *and* he wouldn't *and* he would send somebody for it *and* someone was about to bring it without being asked. Some of the images were drinking coffee, a few had tea or milk, some were smoking, some were leaning too far back with their feet on the desks (and a handful of these were toppling helplessly backward), some were, like this present Trimble, introspecting with their elbows on the desk.

Damn Crosstime anyway.

He'd have had to check Harmon's business affairs, even without the Crosstime link. There might have been a motive there, for suicide or for murder, though it had never been likely.

In the first place, Harmon had cared nothing for money. The Crosstime group had been one of many. At the time that project had looked as hairbrained as the rest: a handful of engineers and physicists and philosophers determined to prove that the theory of alternate time tracks was reality.

In the second place, Harmon had no business worries.

Quite the contrary.

Eleven months ago an experimental vehicle had touched one of the worlds of the Confederate States of America, and returned. The universes of alternate choice were within reach. And the pilot had brought back an artifact.

From that point on, Crosstime travel had more than financed itself. The Confederate world's "stapler," granted an immediate patent, had bought two more ships. A dozen miracles had originated in a single, technologically advanced timeline, one in which the catastrophic Cuba War had been no more than a wet firecracker. Lasers, oxygen-hydrogen rocket motors, computers, strange plastics—the list was still growing. And Crosstime held all the patents.

In those first months the vehicles had gone off practically at random. Now the pinpointing was better. Vehicles could select any branch they preferred. Imperial Russia, Amerindian America, the Catholic Empire, the dead worlds. Some of the dead worlds were hells of radioactive dust and intact but deadly artifacts. From these worlds Crosstime pilots brought strange and beautiful works of art which had to be stored behind leaded glass.

The latest vehicles could reach worlds so like this one that it took a week of research to find the difference. In theory they could get even closer. There was a phenomenon called "the broadening of the bands" . . . .

And that had given Trimble the shivers.

When a vehicle left its own present, a signal went on in the hangar, a signal unique to that ship. When the pilot wanted to return, he simply cruised across the appropriate band of probabilities until he found the signal. The signal marked his own unique present.

Only it didn't. The pilot always returned to find a clump of signals, a broadened band. The longer he stayed away, the broader was the signal band. His own world had continued to divide after his departure, in a constant stream of decisions being made both ways.

Usually it didn't matter. Any signal the pilot chose represented the world he had left. And since the pilot himself had a choice, he naturally returned to them all. But—

There was a pilot by the name of Gary Wilcox. He had been using his vehicle for experiments, to see how close he could get to his own timeline and still leave it. Once, last month, he had returned twice.

Two Gary Wilcoxes, two vehicles. The vehicles had been wrecked: their hulls intersected. For the Wilcoxes it could have been sticky, for Wilcox had a wife and family. But one of the duplicates had chosen to die almost immediately.

Trimble had tried to call the other Gary Wilcox. He was too late. Wilcox had gone skydiving a week ago. He'd neglected to open his parachute.

Small wonder, thought Trimble. At least Wilcox had had motive. It was bad enough, knowing about the other Trimbles, the ones who had gone home, the ones drinking coffee, et cetera. But—suppose someone walked into the office right now, and it was Gene Trimble?

It could happen.

Convinced as he was that Crosstime was involved in the suicides, Trimble (some other Trimble) might easily have decided to take a trip in a Crosstime vehicle. A short trip. He could land *here*.

Trimble closed his eyes and rubbed at the corners with his fingertips. In some other timeline, very close, someone had thought to bring him coffee. Too bad this wasn't it.

It didn't do to think too much about these alternate timelines. There were too many of them. The close ones could drive you buggy, but the ones further off were just as bad.

Take the Cuba War. Atomics had been used, *here,* and now Cuba was uninhabited, and some American cities were gone, and some Russian. It could have been worse.

Why wasn't it? How did we luck out? Intelligent statesmen? Faulty bombs? A humane reluctance to kill indiscriminately?

No. There was no luck anywhere. Every decision was made both ways. For every wise choice you bled your heart out over, you had made all the other choices too. And so it went, all through history.

Civil wars unfought on some worlds were won by either side on others. Elsewhen, another animal had first done murder with an antelope femur. Some worlds were still all nomad; civilization had lost out. If every choice was cancelled elsewhere, why make a decision at all?

Trimble opened his eyes and saw the gun.

That gun, too, was endlessly repeated on endless desks. Some of the images were dirty with years of neglect. Some smelled of gunpowder, fired recently, a few at living targets. Some were loaded. All were as real as this one.

A number of these were about to go off by accident.

A proportion of these were pointed, in deadly coincidence, at Gene Trimble.

See the endless rows of Gene Trimble, each at his desk. Some are bleeding and cursing as men run into the room following the sound of the gunshot. Many are already dead.

Was there a bullet in there? Nonsense.

He looked away. The gun was empty.

Trimble loaded it. At the base of his mind he felt the touch of the *handle*. He would find what he was seeking.

He put the gun back on his desk, pointing away from him, and he thought of Ambrose Harmon, coming home from a late night. Ambrose Harmon, who had won five hundred dollars at poker. Ambrose Harmon, exhausted, seeing the lightening sky as he prepared for bed. Going out to watch the dawn.

Ambrose Harmon, watching the slow dawn, remembering a two thousand dollar pot. He'd bluffed. In some other branching of time, he had lost.

Thinking that in some other branching of time that two thousand dollars included his last dime. It was certainly possible. If Crosstime hadn't paid off, he might have gone through the remains of his fortune in the past four years. He liked to gamble.

Watching the dawn, thinking of all the Ambrose Harmons on that roof. Some were penniless this night, and they had not come out to watch the dawn.

Well, why not? If he stepped over the edge, here and now, another Ambrose Harmon would only laugh and go inside.

If he laughed and went inside, other Ambrose Harmons would fall to their deaths. Some were already on their ways down. One changed his mind too late, another laughed as he fell. . . .

Well, why not? . . . .

Trimble thought of another man, a nonentity, passing a firearms store. Branching of timelines, he thinks, looking in, and he thinks of the man who took his foreman's job. Well, why not? . . . .

Trimble thought of a lonely woman making herself a drink at three in the afternoon. She thinks of myriads of alter egos, with husbands, lovers, children, friends. Unbearable, to think that all the might-have-beens were as real as herself. As real as this ice pick in her hand. Well, why not? . . . .

And she goes out to a movie, but she takes the ice pick.

And the honest citizen with a carefully submerged urge to commit rape, just once. Reading his newspaper at breakfast, and there's another story from Crosstime: they've found a world line in which Kennedy the First was assassinated. Strolling down a street, he thinks of world lines and infinite branchings, of alter egos already dead, or jailed, or President. A girl in a miniskirt passes, and she has nice legs. Well, why not? . . . .

Casual murder, casual suicide, casual crime. Why not? If alternate universes are a reality, then cause and effect are an illusion. The law of averages is a fraud. You can do anything, and one of you will, or did.

Gene Trimble looked at the clean and loaded gun on his desk. Well, why not? . . . .

And he ran out of the office shouting, "Bentley, listen! I've got the answer. . ."

And he stood up slowly and left the office shaking his head. This was the answer, and it wasn't any good. The suicides, murders, casual crimes would continue. . . .

And he suddenly laughed and stood up. Ridiculous! Nobody dies for a philosophical point! . . . .

And he reached for the intercom and told the man who answered to bring him a sandwich and some coffee. . . .

And picked the gun off the newspapers, looked at it for a long moment, then dropped it in the drawer. His hands began to shake. On a world line very close to this one. . . .

And he picked the gun off the newspapers, put it to his head and

fired. The hammer fell on an empty chamber.

fired. The gun jerked up and blasted a hole in the ceiling

fired. The bullet tore a furrow in his scalp.

took off the top of his head.

PASSERBY

It was noon of a hot blue day. The park was lively with raised voices and bright clothing, children and adults and the geriatrics generation, of which I have the honor to be a member. I had come early enough to claim a bench, and was old and feeble enough to hold it.

I had brought a sandwich lunch in a Baggy. I ate slowly, saving out an orange and a second sac of beer for later. The populace danced before me, never dreaming that I was watching.

The afternoon sun burned warm on my scalp. A lizardlike torpor stole over me, so that the sound of adult voices and children's screaming-for-the-hell-of-it dimmed and faded.

But I heard the footsteps. They jarred the earth.

I opened my eyes and saw the rammer.

He was six feet tall and massively built. He wore a scarf and a pair of blue balloon pants, not too far out of style, but they didn't match. What they exposed of his skin was loose on him, as if he had shrunk within it. Indeed, he looked like a giraffe wearing an elephant's skin.

He walked without springs. His feet slapped hard into the gravel with all his weight behind them. Small wonder I had heard him coming. By now everyone in sight was either looking at him, or turning to see what everyone was looking at. Except the children, who had already lost interest.

To me he was irresistible.

There are the casual peoplewatchers who watch their neighbors in restaurants or monorail stations when they have nothing else to do. They develop their own amateurish technique, and they don't know what to look for, and they usually get caught. But I'm not that kind of peoplewatcher.

There are the fanatics, the dedicated ones, who learn their technique in a closed-circuit 3V class. They hold lifetime subscriptions to *Face In The Crowd* and *Eyes Of The City,* the hobby magazines. They write letters to the editor telling how they spotted Secretary-General Haruman in a drug store and he looked unhappy.

That's me.

And here I was not twenty yards from a rammer, a man from the stars.

He had to be that. His taste in clothing was odd, and his carelessly draped skin was alien. His legs had not yet learned to cushion his weight against Earth's heavier gravity. He projected an indefinable combination of discomfort and self-consciousness and interest and surprise and pleasure, that silently shouted: *Tourist!*

His eyes, looking out from behind the ill-fitting mask of his face, were bright and blue and happy. Our staring rudeness was noticed, but did not affect his almost religious joy. Nor did his feet, though they must have hurt. His smile was dreamy and very strange. Lift the corners of a spaniel's mouth with your forefingers, and you'd see such a smile.

He drew in life from the sky and the grass and the voices and the growing things. I watched his face and tried to read it. Was he the priest of some new Earth-worshipping religion? No. Probably he was seeing Earth for the first time: tuning his bio-rhythms to Earth for the first time, feeling Earthweight settle over and into his bones, watching suns rise twenty-four hours apart, until his very genes told him he was home.

It made his day when he saw the boy.

The boy was around ten, a handsome child, naked and tanned all over. (When I was growing up, even the infants wore clothing in public.) I had not noticed him until now, and he in turn had not noticed the rammer. He knelt on the path that passed my bench, his back toward me. I could not see what he was doing; but he was very intent and serious about it.

By now most of the passersby had turned away, from disinterest or an overdose of good manners. I watched the rammer watching the boy. I watched through half-closed eyes, practicing my famous imitation of an old man asleep in the sun. The Heisenberg Principle implies that no peoplewatcher should allow himself to be caught at it.

The boy stooped suddenly, then rose with his hands cupped. Moving with exaggerated care, he turned from the gravel path and crossed the grass toward a dark old oak.

The rammer's eyes went big and round. All his pleasure gave way to horror, and then the horror drained away and left nothing. The star man's eyes turned up in his head, his slack face went even slacker, and his knees began to buckle.

Stiff as I am these days, I reached him. I slid an admittedly bony shoulder under his armpit before he could fall. All the mass of him came gratefully down on me.

I should have folded like an accordion. Somehow I got the rammer to the bench before I had to let go of him. To an astonished matron I wheezed, "Get a doctor!"

She nodded briskly and waddled away. I turned back to the rammer.

Sick eyes looked up at me from under straight black bangs. The rammer's face was oddly tanned: dark where the sun could reach, white as milk where folded skin cast shadows. His chest and arms were like that too. Where the skin was pale it had paled further with shock. "No need for doctor," he whispered. "Not sick. Something I saw."

"Sure. Put your head between your legs. It'll keep you from fainting." I opened my remaining beer sac.

"I will be all right in a moment," he said from between his knees. He spoke the tongue oddly, and his weakness slurred it further. "It was the shock of what I saw."

"Here?"

"Yes. No. Not completely. . . ." He stopped to shift mental gears, and I handed him the beer. He looked at it as if wondering which end to suck on, found the nipple, raised the sac and half-drained it in one desperate draught.

"What was it you saw?" I asked.

He had to finish swallowing. "I saw an alien spacecraft. Without the spacecraft it would have meant nothing."

"What kind of ship? Smithpeople? Monks?" These are the only known spacegoing races, aside from ourselves. I'd never seen one of their ships; but they sometimes docked in the Léshy worlds.

The rammer's eyes narrowed in his quilted face. "I see. You think I speak of some registered alien ship in a human spaceport." His voice was no longer slurred· he picked his words with apparent care. "I was halfway between the Horvendile and Koschei systems, shipwrecked at the edge of lightspeed, waiting to die. And I saw a golden giant walking among the stars."

"A humanoid? Not a ship?"

"I . . . thought it was a ship. I can't prove it."

"Mmm."

"Let me tell you. I was a year and a half out from Horvendile, bound for Koschei. It would have been my first trip home in thirty-one years . . . ."

Flying a ramship under sail is like flying a spiderweb.

Even with the web retracted, a ramship is a flimsy beast. Cargo holds, external cargo netting and hooks, pilot cabin and life support system, and the insystem fusion motor are all contained in a rigid pod just three hundred feet long. All else is balloons and webbing.

At takeoff the balloons are filled with hydrogen fuel for the insystem fusion motor. By the time the ship reaches ramscoop speed the fuel is half gone, replaced by low-pressure gas. The balloons are retained as meteor shielding.

The ramscoop web is superconducting wire, thin as spiderweb, tens of thousands of miles of it. Coiled for takeoff, it forms a roll no bigger than the main pod. Put a uniform negative charge on it and it spreads to form a hoop two hundred miles across. It ripples at first under the differentiating fields. . . .

Interstellar hydrogen, thin as nothing, enters the mouth of the ramscoop web. An atom to a cubic centimeter. Differentiating fields compress it along the axis, compress it until it undergoes fusion. It burns in a narrow blue flame, yellow-tinged at the edges. The electromagnetic fields in the fusion flame begin to support the ramscoop web. Mighty forces add, making web and flame and incoming hydrogen one interlocking whole.

A rigid pod, invisibly small, rides the flank of a wispy cylinder of webbing two hundred miles across. A tiny spider on an enormous web.

Time slows down, distances compress at the higher velocities. Hydrogen flows faster through the web; the ramscoop fields increase in power, the web becomes more rigid, more stable.

A ship should not need supervision as it approaches the midpoint turnover.

"I was halfway to Koschei," said the rammer, "carrying the usual cargo: genetically altered seeds, machine prototypes, spices, and three corpsicles: passengers frozen for storage. We carry anything that cannot be sent by message laser.

"I still don't know what went wrong. I was asleep. I had been asleep for months, with a current pulsing through my brain. Perhaps a piece of meteoric iron entered the ramscoop. Perhaps the hydrogen grew thin for an hour, then thickened too fast. Perhaps we entered a sharply bounded OH+ region. In any case, something twisted the ramscoop field, and the web collapsed.

"I was wakened too late. The web had roman-candled, and was trailing the ship like a parachute that will not open. Wires must have touched, for much of the web was vaporised.

"It was my death," said the rammer. "Without the ramscoop web I was falling helplessly. I would enter the system of Koschei months too early, moving at nearly lightspeed, a dangerous missile. For my honor I must inform Koschei by laser, that I might be shot down before I arrive."

"Take it easy," I soothed him. His jaw had clenched, and the muscles that tightened in his face patterned the skin like a jigsaw puzzle. "Relax. It's all over. Smell the grass; you're on Earth now."

"I wept helplessly at first, though we consider weeping unmanly . . ." The rammer looked around him as if coming awake. "You are right. If I took off my shoes, would the law take offense?"

"No."

He took his shoes off and wiggled his toes in the grass. His feet were too small for him, and his toes were long and agile, almost prehensile.

No doctor had appeared yet. Probably the matronly woman had simply walked away to avoid being involved. In any case, the rammer's strength had returned.

He said, "On Koschei we tend to large girth. Gravity pulls less heavily at the meat of us. To qualify as a rammer I sweated away half my body weight, so that the unneeded two hundred earthweight pounds of me could be replaced by payload cargo."

"You must have wanted the stars badly."

"Yes. I was simultaneously learning disciplines

whose very names most people can neither pronounce nor spell." The rammer pulled at his chin. The quilted skin stretched incredibly, and did not snap back immediately when he let go. "I cut my weight by half, yet my feet hurt when I walk the Earth. My skin has not yet shrunk to fit my smaller mass. Perhaps you noticed."

"What did you do about Koschei?"

"I sent the message. It would precede me to Koschei by just two ship's-months."

"Then?"

"I thought to wait it out, to use what time was left to me. My taped library was adequate . . . but even in the face of death, I grew bored.

"After all, I had seen the stars before. Ahead they were blue-white and thickly clustered. To the side they were orange and red and somewhat sparse. Behind was black space, empty but for a handful of dying embers. Doppler shift made my velocity more than obvious. But there was no sense of *motion*, of *going* somewhere.

"A month and a half of this, and I was ready to go back to sleep.

"When the collision alarm went off, I tried to ignore it. My death was already certain. But the noise bothered me, and I went to the control room to shut it off. I saw then that a respectable mass was approaching, aimed dangerously, from behind.

"From behind! It was moving faster than my own ship! I searched among the sparse crimson dots with my scope at top magnification. Presently I found a golden man walking toward me.

"My first thought was that I had gone mad. My second was that my God had come for me. Then, as the intruder grew in the scope screen, I saw that it was not quite human.

"Somehow that made it better. A golden man walking between the stars was impossible. A golden alien was a lesser impossibility. At least I could examine it sanely.

"I found the alien larger than I had thought, much larger than human.

"It was a biped, definitely humanoid, with two arms and legs and a well-defined head. Its skin glowed like molten gold, all over, for it was hairless and without scales. Between its legs was nothing but smooth skin. Its feet were strange, without toes, and the knee and elbow joints were bulbous and knobby—"

"Were you really thinking in big expansive words like that?"

"I really was. I wanted to forget that I was terrified."

"Oh."

"The intruder was nearing fast. Three times I lowered the magnification. Each time I saw him more clearly. His hands were three fingered, with a long middle finger and two thumbs. The knees and elbows were too far down the limbs, but seemed quite flexible. The eyes—"

"Flexible? You saw them move?"

The rammer became agitated. He stuttered; he had to stop to gain control of himself. When he spoke again he seemed to force the words through his throat.

"I . . . decided that the intruder was not actually walking. But as it approached my ship, it seemed to be walking on empty space."

"Like a robot?"

"Like a not-quite-man. Like a Monk, perhaps, if we could see beneath the garment worn by Monk ambassadors."

"But—"

"Think of a man-sized humanoid." The rammer would not let me interrupt. "Think of him as belonging to a civilization advanced beyond our own. If his civilization had the power, and if he had the power within his civilization, and if he were very egotistical, then perhaps," said the rammer, "perhaps he might command that a spacecraft be built in his own image.

"That is the way I thought of the intruder, in the

ten minutes it took the intruder to reach me. I could not believe that a humanoid with smooth, molten gold skin would evolve in vacuum, nor that he could walk on emptiness. The humanoid shape is for gravity, for planets.

"Where does engineering become art? Once our ground-bound automobiles looked like spacecraft. An advanced spacecraft might be made to look like a given man, and move like him, yet still have the capabilities of a spacecraft. The man himself would ride inside. If a king or millionaire could cause this to be done, why, then he would stride like a god across the stars."

"I wonder if you don't think of yourself in just that way."

The rammer was astonished. "Me? Nonsense. I am a simple rammer. But I find man-shaped spacecraft easier to believe in than golden giants walking on emptiness."

"More comforting, too."

"Yes." The rammer shuddered. "It came up very fast, so that I must damp the magnification to keep him in view. His middle finger was two joints longer than ours, and the thumbs were of different sizes. His eyes were set freakishly far apart, and too low in the head. They glowed red with their own light. His mouth was a wide, lipless horizontal line.

"Not once did I think to avoid the intruder. We could not have reached a collision course by accident. I assumed that he had altered course to follow me, and would alter course again to protect us.

"He was on me before I knew it. I had flipped the magnification down another notch, and when I looked the setting was at zero. I looked up at the sparse red stars, and found a golden dot as it exploded into a golden man.

"I blinked, of course. When my eyes opened he was reaching for me."

"For you?"

The rammer nodded convulsively. "For the pod of

my ship. He was much larger than the pod, or rather, his ship was."

"You still thought it was a ship?" I would not have asked; but he kept changing the pronoun.

"I was looking for windows in the forehead and the chest. I did not find them. He moved like a very large man."

"I hate to suggest it," I said, "not knowing your religion. Could there be gods?"

He jumped as if stung. "Nonsense."

"How about superior beings? If we've evolved beyond the chimpanzees, couldn't—"

"No. Absolutely not," said the rammer. "You don't understand modern xenology. Do you not know that we and the Monks and the Smithpeople are all of equal intelligence? The Smithpeople are not remotely humanoid in shape, yet it makes no difference. When a species begins to use tools, evolution stops."

"I've heard that argument, but—"

"When a species begins to use tools, environment no longer shapes that species. The species shapes its environment to suit itself. Beyond this the species does not develop. It even begins to take care of its feeble-minded and its genetically deficient.

"No, he could have better tools than mine, this intruder, but he could not be my intellectual superior. He was certainly nothing to worship."

"You seem awfully sure of that," I snapped.

Instantly I regretted it; for the rammer shivered and wrapped his arms around his chest. The gesture was ludicrous and pitiful at the same time, for his arms swept up an armful of folded skin and hugged it to him. "I needed to be sure. The intruder had taken my main pod in his hand and pulled me toward—toward his ship.

"I was glad of my crash straps. Without them I'd have bounced about like a pea in a dryer. As it was, I blacked out for an instant. When I opened my eyes I faced a great red iris with a black pupil.

"He looked me over with care. I . . . forced myself to look back. He had no ears, no chin. A bony ridge divided his face where a nose might have been, but there were no nostrils. . . .

"He pulled back for a better view of the main pod. This time I was not jolted. He must have realized that the jolting could hurt me, and done something to prevent it. Perhaps he made his ship inertialess.

"I saw him lift his eyes momentarily to see over my pod.

"You must remember that I was facing back along my own wake, back toward Horvendile, to where most of the stars had been red-shifted to black." The rammer was picking his words with care and patience. They came so slowly that I wanted to squirm. "I was not looking at the stars. But . . . suddenly there were a million clustered stars, and they were all white and bright.

"I did not understand. I put side and forward views on the screen. The stars looked the same in all directtions. Still I did not understand.

"Then I turned back to the intruder. He was walking away across the sky.

"You must understand that as he walked, he receded at much faster than walking speed. Accelerating. In a few seconds he was invisible. I looked for signs of an exhaust, but there was none.

"Then I understood." The rammer lifted his head. "Where is the boy?"

"Boy?"

The rammer looked about him, his blue eyes searching. Children and adults looked back curiously, for he was a weird sight. He said, "I do not see the boy. Could he have left?"

"Oh, *that* boy. Sure, why not?"

"There is something I must see." The rammer eased his weight forward onto his bare and battered feet. I followed him as he crossed the gravel path, followed him onto the grass. And the rammer resumed his tale.

"The intruder had examined me and my ship with care. He had made himself and my ship inertialess, or otherwise cushioned us against acceleration. Then he had cancelled our velocity relative to Koschei."

"But that wasn't enough," I objected. "You'd still die."

The rammer nodded. "Still I was glad to see him go, at first. He was terrifying. And his last mistake was almost a relief. It proved that he was—human is not the word I want. But he could make mistakes."

"Mortal," I said. "He was mortal."

"I do not understand. But never mind. Think of the power of him. In a year and a half, at point six gravities, I had accelerated to a velocity which the intruder cancelled in no more than a second. I preferred death to his dreadful company. At first.

"Then I became afraid. It seemed unjust. He had found me halfway between stars, stranded, waiting to die. He had half-saved me—and then left me to die, no better off than before!

"I searched for him with the scope. Perhaps I could signal him, if I knew where to aim my com laser. . . . But I could not find him.

"Then I became angry. I—" The rammer swallowed. "I screamed insults after him. I blasphemed in seven different religions. The more distant he was, the less I feared him. I was reaching my stride when—when he returned.

"His face was outside my main window, his red eyes looked into mine, his strange hand was reaching for my main pod. My collision alarm was just beginning to sound, it had happened so suddenly. I screamed out —I screamed . . . " He stopped.

"What did you scream?"

"Prayers. I begged for forgiveness."

"Oh."

"He took my ship in his hand. I saw the stars explode in front of me."

We had reached the shade of a dark oak, one so old

and so spread out that its lower limbs needed the support of iron pipes. A family picnicking beneath the tree watched our approach.

"Explode?"

"That lacks accuracy," the rammer apologized. "What happened was this: the stars became very much brighter, at the same time converging toward a point. They flared horribly. I was blinded. The intruder must have shifted me to within a meter-per-second of light-speed.

"I rubbed my hand hard across my eyes. With my eyes closed, I felt acceleration. It remained constant while I waited for my eyes to recover. Through experience I was able to estimate its force at ten meters per second squared."

"But that's—"

"One gravity. When I could see again, I found myself on a yellow plain beneath a glaring blue sky. My pod was red hot, and was already sagging around me."

"Where did he put you?"

"On Earth, in a refertilized part of North Africa. My pod was never built for such things. If Earth's gravity collapsed it, then re-entry should have torn it to pieces. But the intruder must have taken care of that too."

I am a peoplewatcher, an expert. I can crawl into a man's mind without letting him know I exist. I never lose at poker. And I knew the rammer was not lying.

We stood beside the dark oak. The lowermost limb grew almost parallel to the ground, and was supported by three iron pipes. Long as were the rammer's arms, he could not have wrapped them around that limb. Its bark was rough and grey and powdery, and it smelled of dust. The top of it was level with the rammer's chin.

"You're a very lucky man," I said.

"No doubt. What is that?"

Black and furry, an inch and a half long; one end

wiggling in blind curiosity as it moved along the bark.

"A caterpillar. You know, there's no computing the odds you ran against being alive now. You don't seem very cheerful about it."

"I was . . . But think about it," said the rammer. "Think what the intruder must have reasoned out, to do what he did.

"He looked through the main window to examine me as well as he could. I was tied to a chair by crash straps, and his sensors had to see through thick impact quartz designed for transparency in the other direction. He could see me, but only from the front. He could examine the ship, but it was damaged, and he had to guess to what extent.

"First he must have reasoned that I could not slow my ship without the ramscoop web. But he must also have deduced the presence of reserve fuel to decelerate me to zero speed from the lowest speed at which my ramscoop can operate. It is apparent that I must have it. Thus he stopped me dead, or nearly so, and left me to go home the slow way, using only my re-entry reserve fuel.

"After he had left me, he must have realized that I would be dead of age before I ended such a trip. Imagine how thorough his examination of me must have been! So he came back for me.

"By projecting my line of flight he must have known where I was going. But could I live there with a damaged ship? He did not know.

"And so he looked me over more carefully, deduced the star and planet where I must have evolved, and he put me there."

"That's pretty farfetched," I said.

"Yes! The solar system was twelve light-years distant, yet he reached it in an instant! But that is not the point. . . ." The rammer let his voice trail off. He seemed oddly fascinated by the black caterpillar, which was now defying gravity as it explored a vertical wall of bark. "He placed me not only on Earth, but in

North Africa. He deduced not only my planet of origin, but the region where I had evolved.

"I stayed in my pod for two hours before I was found. Your United Nations police took a record of my mind, but they do not believe what they found. A ramship pod cannot be towed to Earth without radar finding it. Further, my ramscoop web is all over the desert. Even the hydrogen balloons survived the re-entry. They think that it must be a hoax, that I was brainwashed as part of that hoax."

"And you? What do you think?"

Again the rammer's face tightened into jigsaw-puzzle lines. "I had convinced myself that the intruder was no more than another spacecraft pilot—a passerby who stopped to help, as some persons will stop to help if your car battery fails far from a city. His power might be greater than mine. He might be wealthier, even within the context of his own culture. We were of different species. Yet he had stopped to help a member of the great brotherhood, for we were both spacemen."

"Because your modern xenology says he couldn't have been your superior."

He didn't answer.

"I can pick a few holes in that theory."

"Can you?"

I ignored his disinterest. "You claim that evolution stops when a species starts building tools. But suppose two tool-users evolved on the same world? Then evolution might go on until one race was dead. We might have had real problems if the dolphins had had hands."

"It may be." He was still watching the caterpillar: an inch and a half of black fur exploring the dark bark. My ear brushed the bark as I faced him, and I smelled the damp wood.

"Then again, not all human beings are alike. There are Einsteins and there are morons. Your passerby might have been of a race that varies more. Make him a super-Einstein—"

"I had not thought of that. I had assumed that his deductions were made with the aid of a computer. At first."

"Then, a species could evolve itself. If they once started fiddling with their genes, they might not stop until their children were mile-high giants with a space drive stuck up their spines. What the *hell* is so interesting about that caterpillar?"

"You did not see what the boy did?"

"Boy? Oh. No, I didn't."

"There was a . . . caterpillar moving along the gravel walk. People passed. None looked down. The boy came, and he stooped to watch."

"Oh!"

"Presently the boy picked up the caterpillar, looked about him, then came here and put the caterpillar safely on the limb."

"And you fainted."

"I should not have been so affected by what, after all, is no more than a comparison. I would have cracked my skull had you not caught me."

"A poor return for the golden one, if you had."

The rammer did not smile. "Tell me . . . if an adult had seen the caterpillar, instead of a boy—"

"Probably he'd have stepped on it."

"Yes, I thought so." The rammer put his tongue in his cheek, which stretched incredibly. "He is nearly upside down. I hope he will not fall off."

"It won't."

"Do you think he is safe there?"

"Sure. Don't worry about it."

FOR A FOGGY NIGHT

The bar was selling a lot of Irish coffee that night. I'd bought two myself. It was warm inside, almost too warm, except when someone pushed through the door. Then a puff of chill, damp fog would roll in.

Beyond the window was grey chaos. The fog picked up all the various city lights: yellow light leaking from inside the bar, passing automobile headlights, white light from frosted street globes, and the rainbow colors of neon signs. The fog stirred all the lights together into a cold grey-white paste and leaked it back through the windows.

Bright spots drifted past at a pedestrian's pace. Cars. I felt sorry for the drivers. Rolling through a grey form-less limbo, running from street globe to invisible street globe, alert for the abrupt, dangerous red dot of a traffic light: an intersection; you couldn't tell other-wise . . . I had friends in San Francisco; there were other places I could be. But it wasn't my city, and I was damned if I'd drive tonight.

A lost night. I'd finished my drink. One more, and I'd cross the street to my hotel.

"You'd best wait until the fog thins out," said the man next to me.

He was a stranger, medium all over; medium height and weight, regular features, manicured nails, feathery brown hair, no scars. The invisible man. I'd never have looked his way if he hadn't spoken. But he was smiling as if he knew me.

I said, "Sorry?"

"The point is, your hotel might not be there when you've crossed the street. Don't be surprised," he added. "I can read minds. We've learned the knack, where I come from."

There are easy ways to interrupt a conversation with a stranger. A blank stare will do it. But I was bored and alone, and a wacky conversation might be just what I needed.

I said, "Why shouldn't my hotel be exactly where I left it?"

He frowned into his scotch-and-soda, then took a swallow. "Do you know the theory of multiple world lines? It seems that whenever a decision is made, it's made both ways. The world becomes two or more worlds, one for each way the decision can go. Ah, I see you know of it. Well, sometimes the world lines merge again."

"But—"

"That's exactly right. The world must split on the order of a trillion times a second. What's so un-believable about that? If you want a real laugh, ask a physicist about furcoated particles."

"But you're saying it's *real*. Every time I get a haircut—"

"One of you waits until tomorrow," said the brown-haired man. "One of you keeps the sideburns. One gets a manicure, one cuts his own nails. The size of the tip varies too. Each of you is as real as the next, and each belongs to a different world line. It wouldn't matter if the world lines didn't merge every so often."

"Uh huh." I grinned at him. "What about my hotel?"

"I'll show you. Look through that window. See the street lamp?"

"Vaguely."

"You bet, vaguely. San Francisco is a town with an active history. The world lines are constantly merging. What you're looking at is the probability of a street lamp being in a particular place. Looks like a big fuzzy ball, doesn't it? That's the locus of points where a bulb might be—or a gas flame. Greatest probability density is in the center, where it shows brightest."

"I don't get it."

"When the world lines merge, everything blurs. The further away something is, the more blurred it looks. I shouldn't say *looks,* because the blurring is real; it's no illusion. Can you see your hotel from here?"

I looked out the appropriate window, and I couldn't. Two hours ago I'd nearly lost my way just crossing the street. Tonight a man could lose himself in any city street, and wander blindly in circles in hopes of finding a curb . . .

"You see? Your hotel's too far away. In the chaos out there, the probability of your hotel being anywhere specific is too small to see. Vanishingly small. You'd never make it."

Something about the way he talked. . . .

"I wondered when you'd notice that." He smiled as if we shared a secret.

"All this time," I said, "I've been thinking that you talk just like everyone else. But you don't. It's not just the trace of accent. Other people don't say *probability density* or *theorem* or *on the order of.*"

"No, they don't."

"Then we must both be mathematicians!" I smiled back at him.

"No," he said.

"But then . . ." But I backed away from the problem, or from the answer. "My glass is empty. Could you use a refill?"

"Thanks, I could."

I fixed it with the bartender. "Funny thing," I told the brown-haired man. "I always thought the blurring effect of fog came from water droplets in the air."

"Bosh," he said. "Bosh and tish. The water's there, all right, whenever the fog rolls in. I can't explain it. The condensation must be a side effect from the blurring of the world lines. But that's not interfering with your vision. Water's transparent."

"Of course. How could I have forgotten that?"

"I forgot it myself, a long time ago." The Scotch was beginning to reach him, I think. He had an accent, and it was growing stronger. "That's why I'm here. That's why I stopped you. Because you'd remember."

The bartender brought us our drinks. His big shoulders were hunched inward against the damp grey light that seeped in the windows.

I sipped at the burning hot glass. Irish whiskey and strong black coffee poured warmth through me, to counteract the cold beyond the walls. A customer departed, and the fog swirled around him and swallowed him.

"I walked into the fog one afternoon," said the brown-haired man. "The fog was thick, like tonight. A cubic mile of cotton, as we say. I was just going out for a pouch of snuff. When I reached the tobacconist's he tried to sell me a bundle of brown paper sticks with a Spanish trade mark."

"Uh huh. What did you do?"

"Tried to get home, of course. Things changed oddly while I wandered in the fog. When it cleared and left me stranded, even my money was no good. The worst of it was that I couldn't even tell my story. Nobody could read my mind to see that I was sane. It was find another fog bank or try to make a life for myself."

"With no money?"

"Oh, I sold my ring and found a poker game."

"Oh, *Oh!*"

"That was a year ago. It's worked out well enough. I thought I might invent something, like the zipper, but that fell through. You're far ahead of us in the physical sciences. But money's no problem. Sometimes there's a fixed horse race. Sometimes I find a poker game, or a crooked crap game where they'll let me bet the right way."

"Sounds great." But not very honest, I thought.

"You disapprove?" My companion's voice had gone thin and cold.

"I didn't say that."

"I compensate for what I take," the brown-haired man said angrily. "I know how to untwist a sick man's mind. If a player sits down with emotional problems, I can help him. If he really needs the money, I can see that it comes to him."

"Why don't you become a psychiatrist?"

He shook his head. "It would take years, and then I'd never be able to hold a patient long enough to do myself any good. He'd get well too fast. Besides that, I *hate* certain people; I'd want to harm them instead of helping them. . . .

"Anyway, I don't go out in the fog any more. I like it here. I stopped you because you're one of those who remember."

"You said that before. What exactly—?"

"After all, people are constantly walking into fogs. Why is it that we don't hear more about people wandering in from alternate world lines? It's because their memories adjust."

"Ah."

"I caught it happening once. A girl from somewhere else . . . I didn't catch the details; they faded too fast. I got her a job as a go-go dancer. I think she was a prize concubine in someone's harem before she ran into the fog.

"Their memories adjust. They forget their friends, their relatives, their husbands and wives in the old world line. They remember what man is king or president or chairman in the new. But not us. You and I are different. I can recognize the rare ones."

"Because you can read minds." Sarcastically. Part of me still disbelieved; yet . . . it fit too well. The brown-haired man talked like a mathematics professor because he was talking to me, and I was a mathematics professor, and he was reading my mind.

He looked thoughtfully into his glass. "It's funny,

how many sense the truth. They won't walk or drive in the fog if they can help it. At the bottom of their minds, they know that they might return home to find a Romish camp, or a Druidic dancing ground, or the center of a city, or a sand dune. You knew it yourself. The top of your mind thinks I'm an entertaining liar. The deepest part of you knew it all before I spoke."

"I just don't like fog," I said. I looked out the window, toward my hotel, which was just across the street. I saw only wet grey chaos and a swirling motion.

"Wait until it clears."

"Maybe I will. Refill?"

"Thanks."

Somehow, I found myself doing most of the talking. The brown-haired man listened, nodded occasionally, asked questions from time to time.

We did not mention fog.

"I need an ordered universe," I said at one point. "Why else would I have studied math? There's never an ambiguity in mathematics."

"Whereas in interpersonal relationships . . ."

"Yes! Exactly!"

"But mathematics is a game. Abstract mathematics doesn't connect with the real universe except by coincidence or convenience. Like the imaginary number system: it's used in circuit design, but it certainly wasn't intended for that."

"No, of course not."

"So that's why you never got married?"

"Right," I said sadly. "Ordered universe. Hey, I never knew that. Did I?"

"No."

The fog cleared about one o'clock. My brown-haired friend accompanied me out.

"Mathematics doesn't fit reality," he was saying. "No more than a game of bridge. The real universe is chaotic."

"Like in-ter-personal re-lationships."

"Maybe you'll find them easier now."

"Like fog. Well, maybe I will. I know some new things about myself . . . where's my hotel?"

There was no hotel across the street.

Suddenly I was cold sober, and cold scared.

"So," said my drinking partner. "You must have lost it earlier. Was it foggy when you crossed?"

"Thick as paste. Oh, brother. Now what do I do?"

"I think the fog's starting to roll in again. Why not wait? The bar won't close until four."

"They close at two in my world." *In my world.* When I admitted that, I made it real.

"Then maybe you should stay in this one. At least the bartender took your money. Which reminds me. Here." He handed me my wallet.

He must have picked my pocket earlier. "For services rendered," he said. "But it looks like you'll need the money."

I was too worried to be angry. "My money passes, but my checks won't. I've got half a term of teaching to finish at Berkeley . . . Tenure, dammit! I've got to get back."

"I'm going to run for it," said the brown-haired man. "Try the fog if you like. You might find your way home." And off he went, running to beat the fog. It was drifting in in grey tendrils as I went back into the bar.

An hour later the fog was a cubic mile of cotton, as they say. I walked into it.

I intended to circle the block where I had left my hotel. But there was no way to get my bearings, and the outlines of the block would not hold still. Sight was gone, sound was strangely altered and muffled. I walked blind and half-deaf, with my arms outstretched to protect my face, treading lightly for fear of being tripped.

One thing, at least, the brown-haired man had failed to warn me about. I walked up to a pedestrian-sized grey blur to ask directions, and when I reached it it wasn't human. It watched me dispassionately as I sidled off.

I might have drifted away from the area. The hotel varied from an ancient barrow to a hot springs (I smelled warm pungent steam) to a glass-sided sky-scraper to a vertical slab of black basalt to an enormous pit with red-glowing rock at the bottom. It never became a hotel.

The mist was turning white with dawn. I heard something coming near: the putt-putt-putt of a motor scooter, but distorted. Distorted to the clop-clop-clop of a horse's hooves . . . and still approaching. It became a pad-pad-pad-pad, the sound of something heavy and catlike. I stood frozen. . . .

The fog blew clear, and the sound was two sets of foot steps, two oddly dressed men walking toward me. It was dawn, and the fog was gone, and I was stranded.

In eerie silence the men took me by the elbows, turned me about and walked me into the building which had been my hotel. It had become a kind of hospital.

At first it was very bad. The attendants spoke an artificial language, very simple and unambiguous, like deaf-mute sign language. Until I learned it, I thought I had been booked into a mental hospital.

It was a retraining center for people who can't read minds.

I was inside for a month, and then an outpatient for another six. Quick progress, they say; but then, I hadn't suffered organic brain damage. Most patients are there because of damage to the right parietal lobe.

It was no trouble to pay the hospital fees. I hold patents on the pressure spray can and the butane lighter. Now I'm trying to design a stapler.

And when the fog is a cubic mile of cotton, as we say, I stay put until it goes away.

WAIT IT OUT

Night on Pluto. Sharp and distinct, the horizon line cuts across my field of vision. Below that broken line is the dim grey-white of snow seen by starlight. Above, space-blackness and space-bright stars. From behind a jagged row of frozen mountains the stars pour up in singletons and clusters and streamers of cold white dots. Slowly they move, but visibly, just fast enough for a steady eye to capture their motion.

Something wrong there. Pluto's rotation period is long: 6.39 days. Time must have slowed for me.

It should have stopped.

I wonder if I may have made a mistake.

The planet's small size brings the horizon close. It seems even closer without a haze of atmosphere to fog the distances. Two sharp peaks protrude into the star swarm like the filed front teeth of a cannibal warrior. In the cleft between those peaks shines a sudden bright point.

I recognize the Sun, though it shows no more disc than any other, dimmer star. The sun shines as a cold point between the frozen peaks; it pulls free of the rocks and shines in my eyes. . . .

The Sun is gone, the starfield has shifted. I must have passed out.

It figures.

Have I made a mistake? It won't kill me if I have. It could drive me mad, though. . . .

I don't feel mad. I don't feel anything, not pain, not

36

loss, not regret, not fear. Not even pity. Just: *what a situation*.

Grey-white against grey-white: the landing craft, short and wide and conical, stands half submerged in an icy plain below the level of my eyes. Here I stand, looking east, waiting.

Take a lesson: this is what comes of not wanting to die.

Pluto was not the most distant planet. It had stopped being that in 1979, ten years ago. Now Pluto was at perihelion, as close to the Sun—and to Earth—as it would ever get. To ignore such an opportunity would have been sheer waste.

And so we came, Jerome and Sammy and I, in an inflated plastic bubble poised on an ion jet. We'd spent a year and a half in that bubble. After so long together, with so little privacy, perhaps we should have hated each other. We didn't. The UN psycho team must have chosen well.

But—just to be out of sight of the others, even for a few minutes. Just to have something to *do*, something that was not predictable. A new world could hold infinite surprises. As a matter of fact, so could our laboratory-tested hardware. I don't think any of us really trusted the Nerva-K under our landing craft.

Think it through. For long trips in space, you use an ion jet giving low thrust over long periods of time. The ion motor on our own craft had been decades in use. Where gravity is materially lower than Earth's, you land on dependable chemical rockets. For landings on Earth and Venus, you use heat shields and the braking power of the atmosphere. For landing on the gas giants—but who would want to?

The Nerva-class fission rockets are used only for takeoff from Earth, where thrust and efficiency count. Responsiveness and maneuverability count for too much during a powered landing. And a heavy planet will always have an atmosphere for braking.

Pluto didn't.

For Pluto, the chemical jets to take us down and bring us back up were too heavy to carry all that way. We needed a highly maneuverable Nerva-type atomic rocket motor using hydrogen for reaction mass.

And we had it. But we didn't trust it.

Jerome Glass and I went down, leaving Sammy Cross in orbit. He griped about that, of course. He'd started that back at the Cape and kept it up for a year and a half. But someone had to stay. Someone had to be aboard the Earth-return vehicle, to fix anything that went wrong, to relay communications to Earth, and to fire the bombs that would solve Pluto's one genuine mystery.

We never did solve that one. Where *does* Pluto get all that mass? The planet's a dozen times as dense as it has any right to be. We could have solved that with the bombs, the same way they solved the mystery of the makeup of the Earth, sometime in the last century. They mapped the patterns of earthquake ripples moving through the Earth's bulk. But those ripples were from natural causes, like the Krakatoa eruption. On Pluto the bombs would have done it better.

A bright star-sun blazes suddenly between two fangs of mountain. I wonder if they'll know the answers, when my vigil ends.

The sky jumps and steadies, and—

I'm looking east, out over the plain where we landed the ship. The plain and the mountains behind seem to be sinking like Atlantis: an illusion created by the flowing stars. We slide endlessly down the black sky, Jerome and I and the mired ship.

The Nerva-K behaved perfectly. We hovered for several minutes to melt our way through various layers of frozen gases and get ourselves something solid to land on. Condensing volatiles steamed around us and boiled below, so that we settled in a soft white glow of fog lit by the hydrogen flame.

Black wet ground appeared below the curve of the landing skirt. I let the ship drop carefully, carefully . . . and we touched.

It took us an hour to check the ship and get ready to go outside. But who would be first? This was no idle matter. Pluto would be the solar system's last outpost for most of future history, and the statue to the first man on Pluto would probably remain untarnished forever.

Jeorme won the toss. All for the sake of a turning coin, Jerome's would be the first name in the history books. I remember the grin I forced! I wish I could force one now. He was laughing and talking of marble statues as he went through the lock.

There's irony in that, if you like that sort of thing.

I was screwing down my helmet when Jerome started shouting obscenities into the helmet mike. I cut the checklist short and followed him out.

One look told it all.

The black wet dirt beneath our landing skirt had been dirty ice, water ice mixed haphazardly with lighter gases and ordinary rock. The heat draining out of the Nerva jet had melted that ice. The rocks within the ice had sunk, and so had the landing vehicle, so that when the water froze again it was halfway up the hull. Our landing craft was sunk solid in the ice.

We could have done some exploring before we tried to move the ship. When we called Sammy he suggested doing just that. But Sammy was up there in the Earth-return vehicle, and we were down here with our landing vehicle mired in the ice of another world.

We were terrified. Until we got clear we would be good for nothing, and we both knew it.

I wonder why I can't remember the fear.

We did have one chance. The landing vehicle was designed to move about on Pluto's surface; and so she had a skirt instead of landing jacks. Half a gravity of thrust would have given us a ground effect, safer and cheaper than using the ship like a ballistic missile. The landing skirt must have trapped gas underneath when the ship sank, leaving the Nerva-K engine in a bubble cavity.

We could melt our way out.

I know we were as careful as two terrified men could be. The heat rose in the Nerva-K, agonizingly slow. In flight there would have been a coolant effect as cold hydrogen fuel ran through the pile. We couldn't use that. But the environment of the motor was terribly cold. The two factors might compensate, or—

Suddenly dials went wild. Something had cracked from the savage temperature differential. Jerome used the damper rods without effect. Maybe they'd melted. Maybe wiring had cracked, or resistors had become superconductors in the cold. Maybe the pile—but it doesn't matter now.

I wonder why I can't remember the fear.

Sunlight—

And a logy, dreamy feeling. I'm conscious again. The same stars rise in formation over the same dark mountains.

Something heavy is nosing up against me. I feel its weight against my back and the backs of my legs. What is it? Why am I not terrified?

It slides around in front of me, questing. It looks like a huge amoeba, sharpless and translucent, with darker bodies showing within it. I'd guess it's about my own weight.

Life on Pluto! But how? Superfluids? Helium II contaminated by complex molecules? In that case the beast had best get moving; it will need shade come sunrise. Sunside temperature on Pluto is all of 50° Absolute.

No, come back! It's leaving, flowing down toward the splash crater. Did my thoughts send it away? Nonsense. It probably didn't like the taste of me. It must be terribly slow, that I can watch it move. The beast is still visible, blurred because I can't look directly at it, moving downhill toward the landing vehicle and the tiny statue to the first man to die on Pluto.

After the fiasco with the Nerva-K, one of us had to go down and see how much damage had been done. That meant tunneling down with the flame of a jet backpack, then crawling under the landing skirt. We didn't talk about the implications. We were probably dead. The man who went down into the bubble cavity was even more probably dead; but what of it? Dead is dead.

I feel no guilt. I'd have gone myself if I'd lost the toss.

The Nerva-K had spewed fused bits of the fission pile all over the bubble cavity. We were trapped for good. Rather, I was trapped, and Jerome was dead. The bubble cavity was a hell of radiation.

Jerome had been swearing softly as he went in. He came out perfectly silent. He'd used up all the good words on lighter matters, I think.

I remember I was crying, partly from grief and partly from fear. I remember that I kept my voice steady in spite of it. Jerome never knew. What he guessed is his own affair. He told me the situation, he told me good-by, and then he strode out onto the ice and took off his helmet. A fuzzy white ball engulfed his head, exploded outward, then settled to the ground in microscopic snowflakes.

But all that seems infinitely remote. Jerome stands out there with his helmet clutched in his hands: a statue to himself, the first man on Pluto. A frost of recondensed moisture conceals his expression.

Sunrise. I hope the amoeba—

That was wild. The sun stood poised for an instant, a white point-source between twin peaks. Then it streaked upward—and the spinning sky jolted to a stop. No wonder I didn't catch it before. It happened so fast.

A horrible thought. What has happened to me could have happened to Jerome! I wonder—

There was Sammy in the Earth-return vehicle, but he couldn't get down to me. I couldn't get up. The life system was in good order, but sooner or later I would freeze to death or run out of air.

I stayed with the landing vehicle about thirty hours, taking ice and soil samples, analyzing them, delivering the data to Sammy via laser beam; delivering also high-minded last messages, and feeling sorry for myself. On my trips outside I kept passing Jerome's statue. For a corpse, and one which has not been prettified by the post-surgical skills of an embalmer, he looks damn good. His frost-dusted skin is indistinguishable from marble, and his eyes are lifted toward the stars in poignant yearning. Each time I passed him I wondered how I would look when my turn came.

"You've got to find an oxygen layer," Sammy kept saying.

"Why?"

"To keep you alive! Sooner or later they'll send a rescue ship. You can't give up now!"

I'd already given up. There was oxygen, but there was no such layer as Sammy kept hoping for. There were veins of oxygen mixed with other things, like veins of gold ore in rock. Too little, too finely distributed.

"Then use the water ice! That's only poetic justice, isn't it? You can get the oxygen out by electrolysis!"

But a rescue ship would take years. They'd have to build it from scratch, and redesign the landing vehicle too. Electrolysis takes power, and heat takes power. I had only the batteries.

Sooner or later I'd run out of power. Sammy couldn't see this. He was more desperate than I was. I didn't run out of last messages; I stopped sending them because they were driving Sammy crazy.

I passed Jerome's statue one time too many, and an idea came.

This is what comes of not wanting to die.

In Nevada, three billion miles from here, half a

million corpses lie frozen in vaults surrounded by liquid nitrogen. Half a million dead men wait for an earthly resurrection, on the day medical science discovers how to unfreeze them safely, how to cure what was killing each one of them, how to cure the additional damage done by ice crystals breaking cell walls all through their brains and bodies.

Half a million fools? But what choice did they have? They were dying.

I was dying.

A man can stay conscious for tens of seconds in vacuum. If I moved fast, I could get out of my suit in that time. Without that insulation to protect me, Pluto's black night would suck warmth from my body in seconds. At 50° Absolute, I'd stay in frozen storage until one version or another of the Day of Resurrection.

Sunlight—

—And stars. No sign of the big blob that found me so singularly tasteless yesterday. But I could be looking in the wrong direction.

I hope it got to cover.

I'm looking east, out over the splash plain. In my peripheral vision the ship looks unchanged and undamaged.

My suit lies beside me on the ice. I stand on a peak of black rock, poised in my silvered underwear, looking eternally out at the horizon. Before the cold touched my brain I found a last moment in which to assume an heroic stance. Go east, young man. Wouldn't you know I'd get my directions mixed? But the fog of my breathing-air hid everything, and I was moving in terrible haste.

Sammy Cross must be on his way home now. He'll tell them where I am.

Stars pour up from behind the mountains. The mountains and the splash plain and Jerome and I sink endlessly beneath the sky.

My corpse must be the coldest in history. Even the

hopeful dead of Earth are only stored at liquid nitrogen temperatures. Pluto's night makes that look torrid,
after the 50° Absolute heat of day seeps away into
space.

A superconductor is what I am. Sunlight raises the
temperature too high, switching me off like a damned
machine at every dawn. But at night my nervous system becomes a superconductor. Currents flow; thoughts
flow; sensations flow. Sluggishly. The one hundred and
fifty-three hours of Pluto's rotation flash by in what
feels like fifteen minutes. At that rate I can wait it out.

I stand as a statue and a viewpoint. No wonder I
can't get emotional about anything. Water is a rock
here, and my glands are contoured ice within me. But
I feel sensations: the pull of gravity, the pain in my ears,
the tug of vacuum over every square inch of my body.
The vacuum will not boil my blood. But the tensions
are frozen into the ice of me, and my nerves tell me so.
I feel the wind whistling from my lips, like an exhala-
tion of cigarette smoke.

This is what comes of not wanting to die. What a
joke if I got my wish!

Do you suppose they'll find me? Pluto's small for a
planet. For a place to get lost in, a small planet is all
too large. But there's the ship.

Though it seems to be covered with frost. Vaporised
gases recondensed on the hull. Grey-white on grey-
white, a lump on a dish of refrozen ice. I could stand
here forever waiting for them to pick my ship from its
surroundings.

Stop that.

Sunlight—

Stars rolling up the sky. The same patterns, endlessly
rolling up from the same points. Does Jerome's corpse
live the same half-life I live now? He should have
stripped, as I did. My God! I wish I'd thought to wipe
the ice from his eyes!

I wish that superfluid blob would come back.

Damn. It's *cold*.

THE JIGSAW MAN

In A.D. 1900, Karl Landsteiner classified human blood into four types: A, B, AB, and O, according to incompatibilities. For the first time it became possible to give a shock patient a transfusion with some hope that it wouldn't kill him.

The movement to abolish the death penalty was barely getting started, and already it was doomed.

Vh83uOAGn7 was his telephone number and his driving license number and his social security number and the number of his draft card and his medical record. Two of these had been revoked, and the others had ceased to matter, except for his medical record. His name was Warren Lewis Knowles. He was going to die.

The trial was a day away, but the verdict was no less certain for that. Lew was guilty. If anyone had doubted it, the persecution had ironclad proof. By eighteen tomorrow Lew would be condemned to death. Broxton would appeal the case on some grounds or other. The appeal would be denied.

The cell was comfortable, small, and padded. This was no slur on the prisoner's sanity, though insanity was no longer an excuse for breaking the law. Three of the walls were mere bars. The fourth wall, the outside wall, was cement padded and painted a restful shade of green. But the bars which separated him from the corridor, and from the morose old man on his left, and from the big, moronic-looking teenager on his

45

right—the bars were four inches thick and eight inches apart, padded in silicone plastics. For the fourth time that day Lew took a clenched fistful of the plastic and tried to rip it away. It felt like a sponge rubber pillow, with a rigid core the thickness of a pencil, and it wouldn't rip. When he let go it snapped back to a perfect cylinder.

"It's not fair," he said.

The teenager didn't move. For all of the ten hours Lew had been in his cell, the kid had been sitting on the edge of his bunk with his lank black hair falling in his eyes and his five o'clock shadow getting gradually darker. He moved his long, hairy arms only at mealtimes, and the rest of him not at all.

The old man looked up at the sound of Lew's voice. He spoke with bitter sarcasm. "You framed?"

"No, I—"

"At least you're honest. What'd you do?"

Lew told him. He couldn't keep the hurt innocence out of his voice. The old man smiled derisively, nodding as if he'd expected just that.

"Stupidity. Stupidity's always been a capital crime. If you *had* to get yourself executed, why not for something important? See the kid on the other side of you?"

"Sure," Lew said without looking.

"He's an organlegger."

Lew felt the shock freezing in his face. He braced himself for another look into the next cell—and every nerve in his body jumped. The kid was looking at him. With his dull dark eyes barely visible under his mop of hair, he regarded Lew as a butcher might consider a badly aged side of beef.

Lew edged closer to the bars between his cell and the old man's. His voice was a hoarse whisper. "How many did he kill?"

"None."

"?"

"He was the snatch man. He'd find someone out alone at night, drug him and take him home to the doc that ran the ring. It was the doc that did all the killing. If Bernie'd brought home a dead donor, the doc would have skinned *him* down."

The old man sat with Lew almost directly behind him. He had twisted himself around to talk to Lew, but now he seemed to be losing interest. His hands, hidden from Lew by his bony back, were in constant nervous motion.

"How many did he snatch?"

"Four. Then he got caught. He's not very bright, Bernie."

"What did you do to get put here?"

The old man didn't answer. He ignored Lew completely, his shoulders twitching as he moved his hands. Lew shrugged and dropped back in his bunk.

It was nineteen o'clock of a Thursday night.

..

The ring had included three snatch men. Bernie had not yet been tried. Another was dead; he had escaped over the edge of a pedwalk when he felt the mercy bullet enter his arm. The third was being wheeled into the hospital next door to the courthouse.

Officially he was still alive. He had been sentenced; his appeal had been denied; but he was still alive as they moved him, drugged, into the operating room.

The interns lifted him from the table and inserted a mouthpiece so he could breathe when they dropped him into freezing liquid. They lowered him without a splash, and as his body temperature went down they dribbled something else into his veins. About half a pint of it. His temperature dropped toward freezing, his heartbeats were further and further apart. Finally his heart stopped. But it could have been started again. Men had been reprieved at this point. Officially the organlegger was still alive.

The doctor was a line of machines with a conveyor belt running through them. When the organlegger's body temperature reached a certain point, the belt started. The first machine made a series of incisions in his chest. Skillfully and mechanically, the doctor performed a cardiectomy.

The organlegger was officially dead.

His heart went into storage immediately. His skin followed, most of it in one piece, all of it still living. The doctor took him apart with exquisite care, like disassembling a flexible, fragile, tremendously complex jigsaw puzzle. The brain was flashburned and the ashes saved for urn burial; but all the rest of the body, in slabs and small blobs and parchment-thin layers and lengths of tubing, went into storage in the hospital's organ banks. Any one of these units could be packed in a travel case at a moment's notice and flown to anywhere in the world in not much more than an hour. If the odds broke right, if the right people came down with the right diseases at the right time, the organlegger might save more lives than he had taken.

Which was the whole point.

Lying on his back, staring up at the ceiling television set, Lew suddenly began to shiver. He had not had the energy to put the sound plug in his ear, and the silent motion of the cartoon figures had suddenly become horrid. He turned the set off, and that didn't help either.

Bit by bit they would take him apart and store him away. He'd never seen an organ storage bank, but his uncle had owned a butcher-shop . . .

"Hey!" he yelled.

The kid's eyes came up, the only living part of him. The old man twisted round to look over his shoulder. At the end of the hall the guard looked up once, then went back to reading.

The fear was in Lew's belly; it pounded in his throat. "How can you stand it?"

The kid's eyes dropped to the floor. The old man said, "Stand what?"

"Don't you know what they're going to *do* to us?"

"Not to me. They won't take me apart like a hog."

Instantly Lew was at the bars. "Why not?"

The old man's voice had become very low. "Because there's a bomb where my right thighbone used to be. I'm gonna blow myself up. What they find, they'll never use."

The hope the old man had raised washed away, leaving bitterness. "Nuts. How could you put a bomb in your leg?"

"Take the bone out, bore a hole lengthwise through it, build the bomb in the hole, get all the organic material out of the bone so it won't rot, put the bone back in. 'Course your red corpuscle count goes down afterward. What I wanted to ask you. You want to join me?"

"Join you?"

"Hunch up against the bars. This thing'll take care of both of us."

Lew had backed up against the opposite set of bars.

"Your choice," said the old man. "I never told you what I was here for, did I? I was the doc. Bernie made his snatches for me."

Lew had backed up against the opposite set of bars. He felt them touch his shoulders and turned to find the kid looking dully into his eyes from two feet away. Organleggers! He was surrounded by professional killers!

"I know what it's like," the old man continued. "They won't do that to me. Well. If you're sure you don't want a clean death, go lie down behind your bunk. It's thick enough."

The bunk was a mattress and a set of springs mounted into a cement block which was an integral part of the cement floor. Lew curled himself into fetal position with his hands over his eyes.

He was sure he didn't want to die *now*.

Nothing happened.

After a while he opened his eyes, took his hands away and looked around.

The kid was looking at him. For the first time there

was a sour grin plastered on his face. In the corridor
the guard, who was always in a chair by the exit, was
standing outside the bars looking down at him. He
seemed concerned.

Lew felt the flush rising in his neck and nose and
ears. The old man had been playing with him. He
moved to get up . . . .

And a hammer came down on the world.

The guard lay broken against the bars of the cell
across the corridor. The lank-haired youngster was
picking himself up from behind his bunk, shaking his
head. Somebody groaned; and the groan rose to a
scream. The air was full of cement dust.

Lew got up.

Blood lay like red oil on every surface that faced
the explosion. Try as he might, and he didn't try very
hard, Lew could find no other trace of the old man.

Except for the hole in the wall.

He must have been standing . . . right . . . there.

The hole would be big enough to crawl through, if
Lew could reach it. But it was in the old man's cell.
The silicone plastic sheathing on the bars between
the cells had been ripped away, leaving only pencil-
thick lengths of metal.

Lew tried to squeeze through.

The bars were humming, vibrating, though there was
no sound. As Lew noticed the vibration he also found
that he was becoming sleepy. He jammed his body between the bars, caught in a war between his rising
panic and the sonic stunners which might have gone
on automatically.

The bars wouldn't give. But his body did; and the
bars were slippery with . . . He was through. He poked
his head through the hole in the wall and looked down.

Way down. Far enough to make him dizzy.

The Topeka County courthouse was a small sky-
scraper, and Lew's cell must have been near the top.
He looked down a smooth concrete slab studded with

windows set flush with the sides. There would be no
way to reach those windows, no way to open them,
no way to break them.

The stunner was sapping his will. He would have
been unconscious by now if his head had been in the
cell with the rest of him. He had to force himself to
turn and look up.

He was *at* the top. The edge of the roof was only
a few feet above his eyes. He couldn't reach that far,
not without . . .

He began to crawl out of the hole.

Win or lose, they wouldn't get him for the organ
banks. The vehicular traffic level would smash every
useful part of him. He sat on the lip of the hole, with
his legs straight out inside the cell for balance, pushing
his chest flat against the wall. When he had his balance
he stretched his arms toward the roof. No good.

So he got one leg under him, keeping the other
stiffly out, and *lunged*.

His hands closed over the edge as he started to fall
back. He yelped with surprise, but it was too late. The
top of the courthouse was moving! It had dragged him
out of the hole before he could let go. He hung on,
swinging slowly back and forth over empty space as
the motion carried him away.

The top of the courthouse was a pedwalk.

He couldn't climb up, not without purchase for his
feet. He didn't have the strength. The pedwalk was
moving toward another building, about the same height.
He could reach it if he only hung on.

And the windows in that building were different.
They weren't made to open, not in those days of
smog and air conditioning, but there were ledges. Perhaps the glass would break.

Perhaps it wouldn't.

The pull on his arms was agony. It would be so easy
to let go. . . . No. He had committed no crime worth
dying for. He refused to die.

Over the decades of the twentieth century the movement continued to gain momentum. Loosely organized, international in scope, its members had only one goal: to replace execution with imprisonment and rehabilitation in every state and nation they could reach. They argued that killing a man for his crime teaches him nothing; that it serves as no deterrent to others who might commit the same crime; that death is irreversible, where as an innocent man may be released from prison if his innocence can be proved. Killing a man serves no good purpose, they said, unless for society's vengeance. Vengeance, they said, is unworthy of an enlightened society.

Perhaps they were right.

In 1940 Karl Landsteiner and Alexander S. Wiener made public their report on the Rh factor in human blood.

By mid-century most convicted killers were getting life imprisonment or less. Many were later returned to society, some "rehabilitated," others not. The death penalty had been passed for kidnapping in some states, but it was hard to persuade a jury to enforce it. Similarly with murder charges. A man wanted for burglary in Canada and murder in California fought extradition to Canada; he had less chance of being convicted in California. Many states had abolished the death penalty. France had none.

Rehabilitation of criminals was a major goal of the science/art of psychology.

But—

Blood banks were world wide.

Already men and women with kidney diseases had been saved by a kidney transplanted from an identical twin. Not all kidney victims had identical twins. A doctor in Paris used transplants from close relatives, classifying up to a hundred points of incompatibility to judge in advance how successful the transplant would be.

Eye transplants were common. An eye donor could

wait until he died before he saved another man's sight.

Human bone could *always* be transplanted, provided the bone was first cleaned of organic matter.

So matters stood in mid-century.

By 1990 it was possible to store any living human organ for any reasonable length of time. Transplants had become routine, helped along by the "scalpel of infinite thinness," the laser. The dying regularly willed their remains to organ banks. The mortuary lobbies couldn't stop it. But such gifts from the dead were not always useful.

In 1993 Vermont passed the first of the organ bank laws. Vermont had always had the death penalty. Now a condemned man could know that his death would save lives. It was no longer true that an execution served no good purpose. Not in Vermont.

Nor, later, in California. Or Washington. Georgia. Pakistan, England, Switzerland, France, Rhodesia . . .

The pedwalk was moving at ten miles per hour. Below, unnoticed by pedestrians who had quit work late and night owls who were just beginning their rounds, Lewis Knowles hung from the moving strip and watched the ledge go by beneath his dangling feet. The ledge was no more than two feet wide, a good four feet beneath his stretching toes.

He dropped.

As his feet struck he caught the edge of a window casement. Momentum jerked at him, but he didn't fall. After a long moment he breathed again.

He couldn't know what building this was, but it was not deserted. At twenty-one hundred at night, all the windows were ablaze. He tried to stay back out of the light as he peered in.

The window was an office. Empty.

He'd need something to wrap around his hand to break that window. But all he was wearing was a pair of shoesocks and a prison jumper. Well, he couldn't be more conspicuous than he was now. He took off the jumper, wrapped part of it around his hand, and struck.

He almost broke his hand.

Well . . . they'd let him keep his jewelry, his wrist-watch and diamond ring. He drew a circle on the glass with the ring, pushing down hard, and struck again with the other hand. It *had* to be glass; if it was plastic he was doomed.

The glass popped out in a near-perfect circle.

He had to do it six times before the hole was big enough for him.

He smiled as he stepped inside, still holding his jumper. Now all he needed was an elevator. The cops would have picked him up in an instant if they'd caught him on the street in a prison jumper, but if he hid the jumper here he'd be safe. Who would suspect a licensed nudist?

Except that he didn't have a license. Or a nudist's shoulder pouch to put it in.

Or a shave.

That was very bad. Never had there been a nudist as hairy as this. Not just a five o'clock shadow, but a full beard all over, so to speak. Where could he get a razor?

He tried the desk drawers. Many businessmen kept spare razors. He stopped when he was halfway through. Not because he'd found a razor, but because he knew where he was. The papers on the desk made it all too obvious.

A hospital.

He was still clutching the jumper. He dropped it in the wastebasket, covered it tidily with papers, and more or less collapsed into the chair behind the desk.

A hospital. He *would* pick a hospital. And *this* hospital, the one which had been built right next to the Topeka County courthouse, for good and sufficient reason.

But he hadn't picked it, not really. It had picked

him. Had he ever in his life made a decision except on the instigation of others? Friends had borrowed his money for keeps, men had stolen his girls, he had avoided promotion by his knack for being ignored. Shirley had bullied him into marrying her, then left him four years later for a friend who wouldn't be bullied.

Even now, at the possible end of his life, it was the same. An aging body snatcher had given him his escape. An engineer had built the cell bars wide enough apart to let a small man squeeze between them. Another had put a pedwalk along two convenient roofs. And here he was.

The worst of it was that here he had no chance of masquerading as a nudist. Hospital gowns and masks would be the minimum. Even nudists had to wear clothing sometime.

The closet?

There was nothing in the closet but a spiffy green hat and a perfectly transparent rain poncho.

He could run for it. If he could find a razor he'd be safe once he reached the street. He bit at a knuckle, wishing he knew where the elevator was. Have to trust to luck. He began searching the drawers again.

He had his hand on a black leather razor case when the door opened. A beefy man in a hospital gown breezed in. The intern (there were no human doctors in hospitals) was halfway to the desk before he noticed Lew crouching over an open drawer. He stopped walking. His mouth fell open.

Lew closed it with the fist which still gripped the razor case. The man's teeth came together with a sharp click. His knees were buckling as Lew brushed past him and out the door.

The elevator was just down the hall, with the doors standing open. And nobody coming. Lew stepped in an punched O. He shaved as the elevator dropped. The razor cut fast and close, if a trifle noisily. He was working on his chest as the door opened.

A skinny technician stood directly in front of him, her mouth and eyes set in the utterly blank expression of those who wait for elevators. She brushed past him with a muttered apology, hardly noticing him. Lew stepped out fast. The doors were closing before he realized that he was on the wrong floor.

That damned tech! She'd stopped the elevator before it reached bottom.

He turned and stabbed the Down button. Then what he'd seen in the one cursory glance came back to him, and his head whipped around for another look.

The whole vast room was filled with glass tanks, ceiling height, arranged in a labyrinth like the bookcases in a library. In the tanks was a display more lewd than anything in Belsen. Why, those things had been *men!* and *women!* No, he wouldn't look. He refused to look at anything but the elevator door. *What was taking that elevator so long?*

He heard a siren.

The hard tile floor began to vibrate against his bare feet. He felt a numbness in his muscles, a lethargy in his soul.

The elevator arrived . . . too late. He blocked the doors open with a chair. Most buildings didn't have stairs: only alternate elevators. They'd have to use the alternate elevator to reach him now. Well, where was it? . . . He wouldn't have time to find it. He was beginning to feel really sleepy. They must have several sonic projectors focused on this one room. Where one beam passed the interns would feel mildly relaxed, a little clumsy. But where the beams intersected, here, there would be unconsciousness. But not yet.

He had something to do first.

By the time they broke in they'd have something to kill him for.

The tanks were faced in plastic, not glass: a very special kind of plastic. To avoid provoking defense reactions in all the myriads of body parts which might be stored touching it, the plastic had to have unique characteristics. No engineer could have been expected to make it shatterproof too!

It shattered very satisfactorily.

Later Lew wondered how he managed to stay up as long as he did. The soothing hypersonic murmur of the stun beams kept pulling at him, pulling him down to a floor which seemed softer every moment. The chair he wielded became heavier and heavier. But as long as he could lift it, he smashed. He was knee deep in nutritive storage fluid, and there were dying things brushing against his ankles with every move; but his work was barely a third done when the silent siren song became too much for him.

He fell.

And after all that they never even mentioned the smashed organ banks!

Sitting in the courtroom, listening to the drone of courtroom ritual, Lew sought Mr. Broxton's ear to ask the question. Mr. Broxton smiled at him. "Why should they want to bring that up? They think they've got enough on you as it is. If you beat *this* rap, then they'll persecute you for wanton destruction of valuable medical sources. But they're sure you won't."

"And you?"

"I'm afraid they're right. But we'll try. Now, Hennessey's about to read the charges. Can you manage to look hurt and indignant?"

"Sure."

"Good."

The prosecution read the charges, his voice sounding like the voice of doom coming from under a thin blond mustache. Warren Lewis Knowles looked hurt and indignant. But he no longer felt that way. He had done something worth dying for.

The cause of it all was the organ banks. With good doctors and a sufficient flow of material in the organ banks, any taxpayer could hope to live indefinitely.

What voter would vote against eternal life? The death penalty was his immortality, and he would vote the death penalty for any crime at all.

Lewis Knowles had struck back.

"The state will prove that the said Warren Lewis Knowles did, in the space of two years, willfully drive through a total of six red traffic lights. During that same period the same Warren Knowles exceeded local speed limits no less than ten times, once by as much as fifteen miles per hour. His record had never been good. We will produce records of his arrest in 2082 on a charge of drunk driving, a charge of which he was acquitted only through—"

"Objection!"

"Sustained. If he was acquitted, Counselor, the Court must assume him not guilty."

NOT LONG BEFORE THE END

A swordsman battled a sorcerer, once upon a time. In that age such battles were frequent. A natural antipathy exists between swordsmen and sorcerers, as between cats and small birds, or between rats and men. Usually the swordsman lost, and humanity's average intelligence rose some trifling fraction. Sometimes the swordsman won, and again the species was improved; for a sorcerer who cannot kill one miserable swordsman is a poor excuse for a sorcerer.

But this battle differed from others. On one side, the sword itself was enchanted. On the other, the sorcerer knew a great and terrible truth.

We will call him the Warlock, as his name is both forgotten and impossible to pronounce. His parents had known what they were about. He who knows your name has power over you, but he must speak your name to use it.

The Warlock had found his terrible truth in middle age.

By that time he had traveled widely. It was not from choice. It was simply that he was a powerful magician, and he used his power, and he needed friends.

He knew spells to make people love a magician. The Warlock had tried these, but he did not like the side effects. So he commonly used his great power to help those around him, that they might love him without coercion.

He found that when he had been ten to fifteen years

in a place, using his magic as whim dictated, his powers would weaken. If he moved away, they returned. Twice he had had to move, and twice he had settled in in a new land, learned new customs, made new friends. It happened a third time, and he prepared to move again. But somthing set him to wondering.

Why should a man's powers be so unfairly drained out of him?

It happened to nations too. Throughout history, those lands which had been richest in magic had been over-run by barbarians carrying swords and clubs. It was a sad truth, and one that did not bear thinking about; but the Warlock's curiosity was strong.

So he wondered, and he stayed to perform certain experiments.

His last experiment involved a simple kinetic sorcery set to spin a metal disc in midair. And when that magic was done, he knew a truth he could never forget.

So he departed. In succeeding decades he moved again and again. Time changed his personality if not his body, and his magic became more dependable if less showy. He had discovered a great and terrible truth; and if he kept it secret, it was through compassion. His truth spelled the end of civilization, yet it was of no earthly use to anyone.

So he thought. But some five decades later (the date was on the order of 12,000 B. C.) it occurred to him that all truths find a use, somewhere, sometime. And so he built another disc, and recited spells over it, so that (like a telephone number already dialled but for one digit) the disc would be ready if ever he needed it.

The name of the sword was Glirendree. It was several hundred years old, and quite famous.

As for the swordsman, his name is no secret. It was Belhap Sattlestone Wirldess ag Miracloat roo Cononson. His friends, who tended to be temporary, called him Hap. He was a barbarian, of course. A civilized man would have had more sense than to touch Glirendree, and better morals than to stab a sleeping woman. Which was how Hap had acquired his sword. Or vice versa.

The Warlock recognized it long before he saw it. He was at work in the cavern he had carved beneath a hill, when an alarm went off. The hair rose up, tingling, along the back of his neck. "Visitors," he said.

"I don't hear anything," said Sharla, but there was an uneasiness to her tone. Sharla was a girl of the village who had come to live with the Warlock. That day she had persuaded the Warlock to teach her some of his simpler spells.

"Don't you feel the hair rising on the back of your neck? I set the alarm to do that. Let me just check . . ." He used a sensor: a slender silver hoop balanced on edge. "There's trouble coming. Sharla, we've got to get you out of here."

"But . . ." Sharla waved protestingly at the table where they had been working.

"Oh, that. We can quit in the middle. That spell isn't dangerous." It was a charm against love-spells, rather messy to work, but safe and tame and effective. The Warlock pointed at the spear of light glaring through the hoop-sensor. "That's dangerous. An enormously powerful focus of manna power is moving up the west side of the hill. You go down the east side."

"Can I help? You've taught me *some* magic."

The magician laughed a little nervously. "Against that? That's Glirendree. Look at the size of the image, the color, the shape. No. You get out of here, and right now. The hill's clear on the eastern slope."

"Come with me."

"I can't. Not with Glirendree loose. Not when it's already got hold of some idiot. There are obligations."

They came out of the cavern together, into the mansion they shared. Sharla, still protesting, donned a robe and started down the hill. The Warlock hastily selected an armload of paraphernalia and went outside.

The intruder was halfway up the hill: a large but apparently human being carrying something long and glittering. He was still a quarter of an hour downslope. The Warlock set up the silver hoop and looked through it.

The sword was a flame of manna discharge, an eye-hurting needle of white light. Glirendree, right enough. He knew of other, equally powerful manna foci, but none were portable, and none would show as a sword to the unaided eye.

He should have told Sharla to inform the Brotherhood. She had that much magic. Too late now.

There was no colored borderline to the spear of light.

No green fringe effect meant no protective spells. The swordsman had not tried to guard himself against what he carried. Certainly the intruder was no magician, and he had not the intelligence to get the help of a magician. Did he know *nothing* about Glirendree?

Not that that would help the Warlock. He who carried Glirendree was invulnerable to any power save Glirendree itself. Or so it was said.

"Let's test that," said the Warlock to himself. He dipped into his armload of equipment and came up with something wooden, shaped like an ocarina. He blew the dust off it, raised it in his fist and pointed it down the mountain. But he hesitated.

The loyalty spell was simple and safe, but it did have side effects. It lowered its victim's intelligence.

"Self defense," the Warlock reminded himself, and blew into the ocarina.

The swordsman did not break stride. Glirendree didn't even glow; it had absorbed the spell that easily.

In minutes the swordsman would be here. The Warlock hurriedly set up a simple prognostics spell. At least he could learn who would win the coming battle.

No picture formed before him. The scenery did not even waver.

"Well, now," said the Warlock. *"Well,* now." And he reached into his clutter of sorcerous tools and found a metal disc. Another instant's rummaging produced a double-edge knife, profusely inscribed in no known language, and very sharp.

At the top of the Warlock's hill was a spring, and the stream from that spring ran past the Warlock's house. The swordsman stood leaning on his sword, facing the Warlock across that stream. He breathed deeply, for it had been a hard climb.

He was powerfully muscled and profusely scarred. To the Warlock it seemed strange that so young a man should have found time to acquire so many scars. But none of his wounds had impaired motor functions. The Warlock had watched him coming up the hill. The swordsman was in top physical shape.

His eyes were deep blue and brilliant, and half an inch too close together for the Warlock's taste.

"I am Hap," he called across the stream. "Where is she?"

"You mean Sharla, of course. But why is that your concern?"

"I have come to free her from her shameful bondage, old man. Too long have you—"

"Hey, hey, hey. Sharla's my *wife.*"

"—Too long have you used her for your vile and lecherous purposes. Too—"

"She stays of her own free will, you nit!"

"You expect me to believe that? As lovely a woman as Sharla, could she love an old and feeble warlock?"

"Do I look feeble?"

The Warlock did not look like an old man. He seemed Hap's age, some twenty years old, and his frame and his musculature were the equal of Hap's. He had not bothered to dress as he left the cavern. In place of Hap's scars his back bore a tattoo in red and green and gold, an elaborately curlicued pentagramic design, almost hypnotic in its extradimensional involutions.

"Everyone in the village knows your age," said Hap. "You're two hundred years old, if not more."

"Hap," said the Warlock. "Belhap something-or-other roo Cononson. Now I remember. Sharla told me you tried to bother her last time she went to the village. I should have done something about it then."

"Old man, you lie. Sharla is under a spell. Everybody knows the power of a warlock's loyalty spell."

"I don't use them. I don't like the side effects. Who wants to be surrounded by friendly morons?" The Warlock pointed to Glirendree. "Do you know what you carry?"

Hap nodded ominously.

"Then you ought to know better. Maybe it's not too late. See if you can transfer it to your left hand."

"I tried that, I can't let go of it." Hap cut at the air, restlessly, with his sixty pounds of sword. "I have to sleep with the damned thing clutched in my hand."

"Well, it's too late then."

"It's worth it," Hap said grimly. "For now I can kill you. Too long has an innocent woman been subjected to your lecherous—"

"I know, I know." The Warlock changed languages suddenly, speaking high and fast. He spoke thus for almost a minute, then switched back to Rynaldese. "Do you feel any pain?"

"Not a twinge," said Hap. He had not moved. He stood with his remarkable sword at the ready, glowering at the magician across the stream.

"No sudden urge to travel? Attacks of remorse? Change of body temperature?" But Hap was grinning now, not at all nicely. "I thought not. Well, it had to be tried."

There was an instant of blinding light.

When it reached the vicinity of the hill the meteorite had dwindled to the size of a baseball. It should have finished its journey at the back of Hap's head. Instead, it exploded a millisecond too soon. When the light had died, Hap stood encircled in a ring of tiny craterlets.

The swordsman's unsymmetrical jaw dropped, and then he closed his mouth and started forward. The sword hummed faintly.

The Warlock turned his back.

Hap curled his lip at the Warlock's cowardice. Then he jumped three feet backward from a standing start. A shadow had pulled itself from the Warlock's back.

In a lunar cave with the sun glaring into its mouth, a man's shadow on the wall might have looked that sharp and black. The shadow dropped to the ground and stood up, a humanoid outline that was less a shape than a window view of the ultimate blackness beyond the death of the universe. Then it leapt.

Glirendree seemed to move of its own accord. It hacked the demon once lengthwise and once across, while the demon seemed to batter against an invisible shield, trying to reach Hap even as it died.

"Clever," Hap panted. "A pentagram on your back, a demon trapped inside."

"That's clever," said the Warlock, "but it didn't work. Carrying Glirendree works, but it's not clever. I ask you again, do you know what you carry?"

"The most powerful sword ever forged." Hap raised the weapon high. His right arm was more heavily muscled than his left, and a touch longer, as if Glirendree had been at work on it. "A sword to make me the equal of any warlock or sorceress, and without the help of demons, either. I had to kill a woman who loved me to get it, but I paid that price gladly. When I have sent you to your just reward, Sharla will come to me—"

"She'll spit in your eye. Now will you listen to me? Glirendree *is* a demon. If you had an ounce of sense, you'd cut your arm off at the elbow."

Hap looked startled. "You mean there's a demon imprisoned in the metal?"

"Get it through your head. *There is no metal.* It's a

demon, a bound demon, and it's a parasite. It'll age you to death in a year unless you cut it loose. A warlock of the northlands imprisoned it in its present form, then gave it to one of his bastards, Jeery of Something-or-other. Jeery conquered half this continent before he died on the battlefield, of senile decay. It was given into the charge of the Rainbow Witch a year before I was born, because there never was a woman who had less use for people, especially men."

"That happens to have been untrue."

"Probably Glirendree's doing. Started her glands up again, did it? She should have guarded against that."

"A year," said Hap. "One year."

But the sword stirred restlesly in his hand. "It will be a glorious year," said Hap, and he came forward.

The Warlock picked up a copper disc. "Four," he said, and the disc spun in midair.

By the time Hap had sloshed through the stream, the disc was a blur of motion. The Warlock moved to keep it between himself and Hap, and Hap dared not touch it, for it would have sheared through anything at all. He crossed around it, but again the Warlock had darted to the other side. In the pause he snatched up something else: a silvery knife, profusely inscribed.

"Whatever that is," said Hap, "it can't hurt me. No magic can affect me while I carry Glirendree."

"True enough," said the Warlock. "The disc will lose its force in a minute anyway. In the meantime, I know a secret that I would like to tell, one I could never tell to a friend."

Hap raised Glirendree above his head and, two-handed, swung it down on the disc. The sword stopped jarringly at the disc's rim.

"It's protecting you," said the Warlock. "If Glirendree hit the rim now, the recoil would knock you clear down to the village. Can't you hear the hum?"

Hap heard the whine as the disc cut the air. The tone was going up and up the scale.

"You're stalling," he said.

"That's true. So? Can it hurt you?"

"No. You were saying you knew a secret." Hap braced himself, sword raised, on one side of the disc, which now glowed red at the edge.

"I've wanted to tell someone for such a long time. A hundred and fifty years. Even Sharla doesn't know." The Warlock still stood ready to run if the swordsman should come after him. "I'd learned a little magic in those days, not much compared to what I know now, but big, showy stuff. Castles floating in the air. Dragons with golden scales. Armies turned to stone, or wiped out by lightning, instead of simple death spells. Stuff like that takes a lot of power, you know?"

"I've heard of such things."

"I did it all the time, for myself, for friends, for whomever happened to be king, or whomever I happened to be in love with. And I found that after I'd been settled for awhile, the power would leave me. I'd have to move elsewhere to get it back."

The copper disc glowed bright orange with the heat of its spin. It should have fragmented, or melted, long ago.

"Then there are the dead places, the places where a warlock dares not go. Places where magic doesn't work. They tend to be rural areas, farmlands and sheep ranges, but you can find the old cities, the castles built to float which now lie tilted on their sides, the unnaturally aged skeletons of dragons.

"So I started wondering."

Hap stepped back a bit from the heat of the disc. It glowed pure white now, and it was like a sun brought to earth. Through the glare Hap had lost sight of the Warlock.

"So I built a disc like this one and set it spinning. Just a simple kinetic sorcery, but with a constant acceleration and no limit point. You know what manna is?"

"What's happening to your voice?"

"Manna is the name we give to the power behind

magic." The Warlock's voice had gone weak and high.

A horrible suspicion came to Hap. The Warlock had slipped down the hill, leaving his voice behind! Hap trotted around the disc, shading his eyes from its heat.

An old man sat on the other side of the disc. His arthritic fingers, half-crippled with swollen joints, played with a rune-inscribed knife. "What I found out—oh, there you are. Well, it's too late now."

Hap raised his sword, and his sword changed.

It was a massive red demon, horned and hooved, and its teeth were in Hap's right hand. It paused, deliberately, for the few seconds it took Hap to realize what had happened, and to try to jerk away. Then it bit down, and the swordsman's hand was off at the wrist.

The demon reached out, slowly enough, but Hap in his surprise was unable to move. He felt the taloned fingers close his windpipe.

He felt the strength leak out of the taloned hand, and he saw surprise and dismay spread across the demon's face.

The disc exploded. All at once and nothing first, it disintegrated into a flat cloud of metallic particles and was gone, flashing away as so much meteorite dust. The light was as lightning striking at one's feet. The sound was its thunder. The smell was vaporized copper.

The demon faded, as a chameleon fades against its background. Fading, the demon slumped to the ground in slow motion, and faded further, and was gone. When Hap reached out with his foot, he touched only dirt.

Behind Hap was a trench of burnt earth.

The spring had stopped. The rocky bottom of the stream was drying in the sun.

The Warlock's cavern had collapsed. The furnishings of the Warlock's mansion had gone crashing down into that vast pit; but the mansion itself was gone without trace.

Hap clutched his messily severed wrist, and he said, "But what happened?"

"Manna," the Warlock mumbled. He spat out a complete set of blackened teeth. "Manna. What I discovered was that the power behind magic is a natural resource, like the fertility of the soil. When you use it up, it's gone."

"But—"

"Can you see why I kept it a secret? One day all the wide world's manna will be used up. No more manna, no more magic. Do you know that Atlantis is tectonically unstable? Succeeding sorcerer-kings renew the spells each generation to keep the whole continent from sliding into the sea. What happens when the spells don't work any more? They couldn't possibly evacuate the whole continent in time. Kinder not to let them know."

"But . . . that disc."

The Warlock grinned with his empty mouth and ran his hands through snowy hair. All the hair came off in his fingers, leaving his scalp bare and mottled. "Senility is like being drunk. The disc? I told you. A kinetic sorcery with no upper limit. The disc keeps accelerating until all the manna in the locality has been used up."

Hap moved a step forward. Shock had drained half his strength. His foot came down jarringly, as if all the spring were out of his muscles.

"You tried to kill me."

The Warlock nodded. "I figured if the disc didn't explode and kill you while you were trying to go around it, Glirendree would strangle you when the constrainment wore off. What are you complaining about? It cost you a hand, but you're free of Glirendree."

Hap took another step, and another. His hand was beginning to hurt, and the pain gave him strength. "Old man," he said thickly. "Two hundred years old. I can break your neck with the hand you left me. And I will."

The Warlock raised the inscribed knife.

"That won't work. No more magic." Hap slapped

the Warlock's hand away and took the Warlock by his bony throat.

The Warlock's hand brushed easily aside, and came back, and up. Hap wrapped his arms around his belly and backed away with his eyes and mouth wide open. He sat down hard.

"A knife always works," said the Warlock.

"Oh," said Hap.

"I worked the metal myself, with ordinary blacksmith's tools, so the knife wouldn't come apart. The runes aren't magic. They only say—"

"Oh," said Hap. "Oh." He toppled sideways.

The Warlock lowered himself onto his back. He held the knife up and read the markings, in a language only the Brotherhood remembered.

AND THIS, TOO, SHALL PASS AWAY. It was a very old platitude, even then.

He dropped his arm back and lay looking at the sky.

Presently the blue was blotted by a shadow.

"I told you to get out of here," he whispered.

"You should have known better. What's *happened* to you?"

"No more youth spells. I knew I'd have to do it when the prognostics spell showed blank." He drew a ragged breath. "It was worth it. I killed Glirendree."

"Playing hero, at your age! What can I do? How can I help?"

"Get me down the hill before my heart stops. I never told you my true age—"

"I knew. The whole village knows." She pulled him to sitting position, pulled one of his arms around her neck. It felt dead. She shuddered, but she wrapped her own arm around his waist and gathered herself for the effort. "You're so thin! Come on, love. We're going to stand up." She took most of his weight onto her, and they stood up.

"Go slow. I can hear my heart trying to take off."

"How far do we have to go?"

"Just to the foot of the hill, I think. Then the spells

will work again, and we can rest." He stumbled. "I'm going blind," he said.

"It's a smooth path, and all downhill."

"That's why I picked this place. I knew I'd have to use the disc someday. You can't throw away knowledge. Always the time comes when you use it, because you have to, because it's there."

"You've changed so. So— so ugly. And you smell."

The pulse fluttered in his neck, like a hummingbird's wings. "Maybe you won't want me, after seeing me like this."

"You can change back, can't you?"

"Sure. I can change to anything you like. What color eyes do you want?"

"I'll be like this myself someday," she said. Her voice held cool horror. And it was fading; he was going deaf.

"I'll teach you the proper spells, when you're ready. They're dangerous. Blackly dangerous."

She was silent for a time. Then: "What color were *his* eyes? You know, Belhap Sattlestone whatever."

"Forget it," said the Warlock, with a touch of pique.

And suddenly his sight was back.

But not forever, thought the Warlock as they stumbled through the sudden daylight. When the manna runs out I'll go like a blown candle flame, and civilization will follow. No more magic, no more magic-based industries. Then the whole world will be barbarians until men learn a new way to coerce nature, and the swordsmen, the damned stupid swordsmen will win after all.

UNFINISHED STORY # 1

As he left the blazing summer heat outside the Warlock's cave, the visiting sorcerer sighed with pleasure. "Warlock, how can you keep the place so cool? The manna in this region has decreased to the point where magic is nearly impossible."

The Warlock smiled—and so did the unnoticeable young man who was sorting the Warlock's parchments in a corner of the cave. The Warlock said, "I used a very *small* demon, Harlaz. He was generated by a simple, trivial spell. His intelligence is low—fortunately, for his task is a dull one. He sits at the entrance to this cave and prevents the fast-moving molecules of air from entering and the slow-moving molecules from leaving. The rest he lets pass. Thus the cave remains cool."

"That's marvelous, Warlock! I suppose the process can be reversed in winter?"

"Of course."

"Ingenious."

"Oh, I didn't think of it," the Warlock said hastily. "Have you met my clerk? It was his idea." The Warlock raised his voice. "Oh, Maxwell

UNFINISHED STORY # 2

There are some things Man was not meant to know.

MAN OF STEEL
WOMAN OF KLEENEX

He's faster than a speeding bullet. He's more powerful than a locomotive. He's able to leap tall buildings at a single bound. Why can't he get a girl?

At the ripe old age of thirty-one*, Kal-El (alias Superman, alias Clark Kent) is still unmarried. Almost certainly he is still a virgin. This is a serious matter. The species itself is in danger!

An unwed Superman is a mobile Superman. Thus it has been alleged that those who chronicle the Man of Steel's adventures are responsible for his condition. But the cartoonists are not to blame.

Nor is Superman handicapped by psychological problems.

Granted that the poor oaf is not entirely sane. How could he be? He is an orphan, a refugee, and an alien. His homeland no longer exists in any form, save for gigatons upon gigatons of dangerous, prettily colored rocks.

As a child and young adult, Kal-El must have been hard put to find an adequate father-figure. What human could control his antisocial behavior? What human would dare try to punish him? His actual, highly social behavior during this period indicates an inhuman self-restraint.

* Superman first appeared in *Action Comics*, June 1938.

What wonder if Superman drifted gradually into schizophrenia? Torn between his human and kryptonian identities, he chose to be both, keeping his split personalities rigidly separate. A psychotic desperation is evident in his defense of his "secret identity."

But Superman's sex problems are strictly physiological, and quite real.

The purpose of this article is to point out some medical drawbacks to being a kryptonian among human beings, and to suggest possible solutions. The kryptonian humanoid must not be allowed to go the way of the pterodactyl and the passenger pigeon.

I

What turns on a kryptonian?

Superman is an alien, an extraterrestrial. His humanoid frame is doubtless the result of parallel evolution, as the marsupials of Australia resemble their mammalian counterparts. A specific niche in the ecology calls for a certain shape, a certain size, certain capabilities, certain eating habits.

Be not deceived by appearances. Superman is no relative to homo sapiens.

What arouses Kal-El's mating urge? Did kryptonian women carry some subtle mating cue at appropriate times of the year? Whatever it is, Lois Lane probably doesn't have it. We may speculate that she smells wrong, less like a kryptonian woman than like a terrestrial monkey. A mating between Superman and Lois Lane would feel like sodomy—and would be, of course, by church and common law.

II

Assume a mating between Superman and a human woman, designated LL for convenience.

Either Superman has gone completely schizo and believes himself to be Clark Kent; or he knows what he's doing, but no longer gives a damn. Thirty-one years is a long time. For Superman it has been even longer. He has X-ray vision; he knows just what he's missing.*

The problem is this. Electroencephalograms taken of men and women during sexual intercourse show that orgasm resembles "a kind of pleasurable epileptic attack." One loses control over one's muscles.

Superman has been known to leave his fingerprints in steel and in hardened concrete, accidentally. What would he do to the woman in his arms during what amounts to an epileptic fit?

III

Consider the driving urge between a man and a woman, the monomaniacal urge to achieve greater and greater penetration. Remember also that we are dealing with kryptonian muscles.

Superman would literally crush LL's body in his arms, while simultaneously ripping her open from crotch to sternum, gutting her like a trout.

IV

Lastly, he'd blow off the top of her head.

Ejaculation of semen is entirely involuntary in the human male, and in all other forms of terrestrial life. It would be unreasonable to assume otherwise for a kryptonian. But with kryptonian muscles behind it,

---

* One should not think of Superman as a Peeping Tom. A biological ability must be used. As a child Superman may never have known that things had surfaces, until he learned to suppress his X-ray vision.

If millions of people tend shamelessly to wear clothing with no lead in the weave, that is hardly Superman's fault.

Kal-El's semen would emerge with the muzzle velocity of a machine gun bullet.*

In view of the foregoing, normal sex is impossible between LL and Superman.

Artificial insemination may give us better results.

V

First we must collect the semen. The globules will emerge at transsonic speeds. Superman must first ejaculate, then fly frantically after the stuff to catch it in a test tube. We assume that he is on the Moon, both for privacy and to prevent the semen from exploding into vapor on hitting air at such speeds.

He can catch the semen, of course, before it evaporates in vacuum. He's faster than a speeding bullet.

But can he keep it?

All known forms of kryptonian life have superpowers. The same must hold true of living kryptonian sperm. We may reasonably assume that kryptonian sperm are vulnerable only to starvation and to green kryptonite; that they can travel with equal ease through water, air, vacuum, glass, brick, boiling steel, solid steel, liquid helium or the core of a star; and that they are capable of translight velocities.

What kind of a test tube will hold such beasties?

Kryptonian sperm and their unusual powers will give us further trouble. For the moment we will assume (because we must) that they tend to stay in the seminal fluid, which tends to stay in a simple glass tube. Thus Superman and LL can perform artificial insemination.

At least there will be another generation of kryptonians.

Or will there?

* One can imagine that the Kent home in Smallville was riddled with holes during Superboy's puberty. And why did Lana Lang never notice *that*?

VI

A ripened but unfertilized egg leaves LL's ovary, begins its voyage down her Fallopian tube.

Some time later, tens of millions of sperm, released from a test tube, begin their own voyage up LL's Fallopian tube.

The magic moment approaches . . .

Can human breed with kryptonian? Do we even use the same genetic code? On the face of it, LL could more easily breed with an ear of corn than with Kal-El. But coincidence does happen. If the genes match . . .

One sperm arrives before the others. It penetrates the egg, forms a lump on its surface. The cell wall now thickens to prevent other sperm from entering. Within the now-fertilized egg, changes take place . . .

And ten million kryptonian sperm arrive slightly late.

Were they human sperm, they would be out of luck. But these tiny blind things are more powerful than a locomotive. A thickened cell wall won't stop them. They will *all* enter the egg, obliterating it entirely in an orgy of microscopic gang rape. So much for artificial insemination.

But LL's problems are just beginning.

VII

Within her body there are still tens of millions of frustrated kryptonian sperm. The single egg is now too diffuse to be a target. The sperm scatter.

They scatter without regard to what is in their path. They leave curved channels, microscopically small. Presently all will have found their way to the open air.

That leaves LL with several million microscopic perforations all leading deep into her abdomen. Most of the channels will intersect one or more loops of intestine.

Peritonitis is inevitable. LL becomes desperately ill.

Meanwhile, tens of millions of sperm swarm in the air over Metropolis.

VIII

This is more serious than it looks.

Consider: these sperm are virtually indestructible. Within days or weeks they will die for lack of nourishment. Meanwhile they cannot be affected by heat, cold, vacuum, toxins, or anything short of green kryptonite.* There they are, miniscule but dangerous; for each has supernormal powers.

Metropolis is shaken by tiny sonic booms. Wormholes, charred by meteoric heat, sprout magically in all kinds of things: plate glass, masonry, antique ceramics, electric mixers, wood, household pets, and citizens. Some of the sperm will crack lightspeed. The Metropolis night comes alive with a network of narrow, eerie blue lines of Cherenkov radiation.

And women whom Superman has never met find themselves in a delicate condition.

Consider: LL won't get pregnant because there were too many of the blind mindless beasts. But whenever one sperm approaches an unfertilized human egg in its panic flight, it will attack.

How close is close enough? A few centimeters? Are sperm attracted by chemical cues? It seems likely. Metropolis had a population of millions; and a kryptonian sperm could travel a long and crooked path, billions of miles, before it gives up and dies.

* And other forms of kryptonite. For instance, there are chunks of red kryptonite that make giants of kryptonians. Imagine ten million earthworm-sized spermatozoa swarming over a Metropolis beach, diving to fertilize the beach balls . . . but I digress.

Several thousand blessed events seem not unlikely.*

Several thousand lawsuits would follow. Not that Superman can't afford to pay. There's a trick where you squeeze a lump of coal into its allotropic diamond form. . .

IX

The above analysis gives us part of the answer. In our experiment in artificial insemination, we must use a single sperm. This presents no difficulty. Superman may use his microscopic vision and a pair of tiny tweezers to pluck a sperm from the swarm.

X

In its eagerness the single sperm may crash through LL's abdomen at transsonic speeds, wreaking havoc. Is there any way to slow it down?

There is. We can expose it to gold kryptonite.

Gold kryptonite, we remember, robs a kryptonian of all of his supernormal powers, permanently. Were we to expose Superman himself to gold kryptonite, we would solve all his sex problems, but he would be Clark Kent forever. We may regard this solution as somewhat drastic.

But we can expose the test tube of seminal fluid to gold kryptonite, then use standard techniques for artificial insemination.

By any of these methods we can get LL pregnant, without killing her. Are we out of the woods yet?

---

* If the pubescent Superboy plays with himself, we have the same problem over Smallville.

XI

Though exposed to gold kryptonite, the sperm still carries kryptonian genes. If these are recessive, then LL carries a developing human foetus. There will be no more Supermen; but at least we need not worry about the mother's health.

But if some or all of the kryptonian genes are dominant. . .

Can the infant use his X-ray vision before birth? After all, with such a power he can probably see through his own closed eyelids. That would leave LL sterile. If the kid starts using heat vision, things get even worse.

But when he starts to kick, it's all over. He will kick his way out into the open air, killing himself and his mother.

XII

Is there a solution?

There are several. Each has drawbacks.

We can make LL wear a kryptonite* belt around her waist. But too little kryptonite may allow the child to damage her, while too much may damage or kill the child. Intermediate amounts may do both! And there is no safe way to experiment.

A better solution is to find a host-mother.

We have not yet considered the existence of Super-

---

* For our purposes, all forms of kryptonite are available in unlimited quantities. It has been estimated, from the startling tonnage of kryptonite fallen to Earth since the explosion of krypton, that the planet must have outweighed our entire solar system. Doubtless the "planet" Krypton was a cooling black dwarf star, one of a binary pair, the other member being a red giant.

girl.* She could carry the child without harm. But Supergirl has a secret identity, and her secret identity is no more married than Supergirl herself. If she turned up pregnant, she would probably be thrown out of school.

A better solution may be to implant the growing foetus in Superman himself. There are places in a man's abdomen where a foetus could draw adequate nourishment, growing as a parasite, and where it would not cause undue harm to surrounding organs. Presumably Clark Kent can take a leave of absence more easily than Supergirl's schoolgirl alter ego.

When the time comes, the child would be removed by Caesarian section. It would have to be removed early, but there would be no problem with incubators as long as it was fed. I leave the problem of cutting through Superman's invulnerable skin, as an exercise for the alert reader.

The mind boggles at the image of a pregnant Superman cruising the skies of Metropolis. Batman would refuse to be seen with him; strange new jokes would circulate the prisons . . . and the race of Krypton would be safe at last.

---

*She can't mate with Superman because she's his first cousin. And only a cad would suggest differently.

EXERCISE IN SPECULATION:
THE THEORY AND PRACTICE
OF TELEPORTATION

Why teleportation? Well—

The regional fan convention, known as Boskone and held annually in Boston had chosen me as Guest of Honor. Strangely, everyone seemed to expect a speech. I hadn't done any speaking since early college. Worse, the audience was jammed with MIT students.

Why teleportation? Because that way none of the MITSFS (MIT Science Fiction Association, pronounced "misfits") could catch me at anything. What with no firm ground for believing that teleportation is even possible, there would be endless room for speculation without any way for some teenage genius to tell me, "You're wrong! Right here in my physics text it says—"

At that, there was enough argument. But the speech went well, even to the point where the question session degenerated into frenzied arguments near the back wall, allowing me to slip quietly away. I'd planned that. But Fred Pohl caught me at the door and asked me to turn the speech into an article for him. Here it is.

DISCLAIMER: Any resemblance to the plots of ancient or modern science fiction, novels or short stories, is *not* coincidence. I've been reading science fiction, voraciously, for eighteen years. In most of what follows, I have borrowed freely from my betters, and even from my own stories. Where I remember my sources, I have quoted them—sometimes.

DEFINITION: Teleportation is any method of moving from point to point in negligible time. Over short distances we will take lightspeed as negligible. Over longer distances (interplanetary and interstellar) we will require infinite or near-infinite speed.

I make a distinction between psychic and mechanical—teleportation. Essentially, psi teleportation involves wishing oneself from place to place. In mechanical teleportation he pushes a button. He may do other things first, such as sighting in, charging batteries, weighing and measuring his cargo, whatever it takes. But eventually he will push a button *here* and he will instantly be *there*. Similarly, the adept at psi teleportation may have spent decades in spiritual training, learning to negate distance by the power of a wish.

These definitions are not meant to be rigorous. Intuitively you know what teleportation is anyway.

HISTORY: The history of teleportation is all of the psi variety. Naturally.

The prophet Elijah was frequently "transported" by Jahweh. He would rise in the air, spin around a few times, and then vanish. Or he would fly about and come down without vanishing. One day he flew up and up and never did come down. His followers searched the countryside for days. When they couldn't find his body they assumed that Elijah had taken it with him, into Heaven.

Friar Joseph of Copertino (1603–1663) was a levitator. Usually in the presence of witnesses, he would go into a religious trance, rise into the air, fly about, eventually settle on an altar or in a tree. His presence in this article derives from his power of bilocation. Friar Joseph was capable of being in two places at once.

Then there are past and present Hindu mystics, and tales of teleportation during séances. No matter. The interesting thing is that, historically, nobody seems to make a distinction between negating distance with a wish, flying by flapping one's arms, flying *without* flapping one's arms, being in two places at once, or being blown about at teriffic speeds by divine or other mysterious forces. The distinction seems to be original with science fiction; it has no basis in recorded "fact".

I offer the thought that there may be no distinction; that this confusion may be a fundamental characteristic of psychic teleportation.

THEORY OF PSYCHIC TELEPORTATION: I'd like to get through this fairly quickly, since I don't believe in psi teleportation, and since my major interest is in the effects of teleportation on society.

1) Consider the following theory: *A man in deadly danger would learn to teleport in order to save his life.*

I can remember two novels in which the idea was crucial: JACK OF EAGLES, by James Blish, and THE STARS MY DESTINATION, by Alfred Bester. The idea is simply to point a gun at a man's head, and fire. One time out of a thousand he will frantically teleport out of the way of the bullet, and you will have a teleport.

Forget it. There has been too much opportunity for it! Violent death has occurred since man was definably man. How many have learned to teleport in time to save their lives? Too few to be noticed.

But there's another flaw in the theory. Psychic powers are notoriously undependable. Experience says that when the ability to teleport is most needed, that's when it won't show up.

2) My prejudice against teleportation has a valid basis. I haven't seen it in action.

Science has existed on Earth for—depending on how you define science—between a couple of centuries and a few millenia. We can't yet build a hardware-type teleport system. But psi powers, if they exist at all, have been around since man was definably human. If teleportation is both possible and useful, we should have been using it since men moved into the Nile Valley. And we would never have given it up . . . if teleportation is *both* possible *and* useful.

We conclude either that teleportation is not possible, or that it kills those who possess the gift before they can demonstate it to anyone. Both are possible.

Consider Bester's "Blue Jaunt". A man in a panic, drowning, teleports without considering where he's going. He ends up inside a wall. BOOM! Bad trip.

Or, psi could be dangerous in other ways. Gene-linked to insanity or to mental deficiency, for example.

In any case, psi teleportation is out. But let's ignore facts and do some speculating.

PRACTICE OF PSYCHIC TELEPORTATION: What about conservation of energy? What of conservation of momentum?

These questions are not idle. Stones did not stop falling when Einstein published a new theory of gravitation. The old laws hold; new laws of physics usually apply only to new areas of observation. Changing one physical law is like trying to eat one peanut.

Okay. So what happens if you try to teleport uphill? Does your body get colder, or lose mass? There is a gain in potential energy. It must be compensated by the loss of energy of another form.

Suppose I were to teleport to Kerguelen Island? (I am writing in Los Angeles. Opposite me on the Earth's globe is the heart of the Indian Ocean, in which Kerguelen Island is the nearest land mass.) Because of the Earth's spin, Los Angeles and Kerguelen Island are going in opposite directions. Were I to teleport to Kerguelen Island I would have to land running—at half a mile a second.

Teleportation can be dangerous. You don't teleport out of a speeding car either.

3) I take another theory of psi teleportation from THE WORLD OF Ā, by A. E. Van Vogt. It seems that two objects similar to each other, to twenty decimal places will join each other. The lesser will bridge space to contact the greater. This presumed law applies to masses, thought waves, and even whole personalities.

We can't disprove it. It could be a fact. We can't disprove it because Van Vogt never defined similarity, nor greater, nor lesser. So now you know how to write a science fiction story. But we can still work with the idea; and I believe Van Vogt missed some great comic routines. Take this one:

In one scene in THE PAWNS OF Ā, we see Gilbert Gosseyn on one side of a fence. He wants to be on the other. So he looks at a piece of land just beyond the fence and, with the power of his extraordinary brain, he tunes himself to that piece of land, adjusting his own atomic makeup to a similarity of within twenty decimal places.

Now, twenty decimal places is pretty finicky. Gosseyn must get within that range, but he must also make sure that he will be the lesser of the pair, and not the greater. One slightest slip . . .

So he makes the bridge . . . and half a ton of earth descends on him.

I don't believe in psychic teleportation. But I could be wrong. So:

We will assume that it is possible for nearly anyone to learn to teleport. A new learning technique has been developed. It may be serving DNA or RNA molecules in one's food, tailoring them to carry a superficial memory directly to the brain, as we now feed flatworms to each other to transfer learned responses. It may be something else. What do you get, when nearly everyone on Earth can teleport?

You get Alfred Bester's THE STARS MY DESTINATION. I offer the book as a text to accompany this course. I'll name a few highlights:

Thieves, uncatchable or nearly so, who teleport around the world to follow the night. They never see sunlight.

Locked doors, and behind the doors, mazes complex enough to confuse anyone who might try to teleport inside. Otherwise there would be no private property, nor privacy either.

Transport vehicles become obsolete. Collectors collect them as period pieces.

Classification of each citizen's teleport characteristics. (Bester assumes a distance limit. My own question: is the limit due to relativistic uncertainty? The more distant is one's destination, the less certain is its location in space and time.)

Intensive, probably productive research into other psi powers (since one has been shown to exist).

I object to one thread of Bester's tapestry. If Gully Foyle tries to "jaunt" along a "geodesic curve" he will end by going slower than light. That's how geodesics work in Einsteinian space. But it doesn't affect the pattern of Bester's society, which is worth studying.

THEORY OF MECHANICAL TELEPORTATION: Anyone know anything about tunnel diodes?

The field is full of good writers named Smith. One wrote a story using a teleportation system based on the tunnel diode effect. Apparently physics students are now taught that a tunnel diode takes an electron *here* and puts it *there* without allowing it to occupy the intervening space. If you can do it with quantum physics, why not with larger masses? With people? The theory looks good, and it hasn't been used much in science fiction.

Older, more often used, and more traditional is the beaming method. You convert your passenger and/or cargo to electromagnetic waves, fire the beam across space, catch it in a receiver and convert the electromagnetic energy back into matter.

A modification is Poul Anderson's system in THE ENEMY STARS. Poul's system records the position and energy state of every subatomic particle in the passenger's body. A side effect is that the body is vaporized, so that one winds up with a complete record of the passenger plus a cloud of superheated plasma. The gas is sucked down through a grid, into a matter reserve, to await the next incoming signal.

The record of the passenger is fired across space.

A receiver picks it up and uses it, plus the plasma in its own matter reserve, to reconstruct the passenger.

I don't know. I wouldn't ride in one of the goddamned things.

The engineering problems seem trivial compared to the legal, ethical, and philosophical ramifications. Still, what happens if the signal gets snarled up? In the good old days I read of the possibilities in EC comic books; and the pictures were vivid and horrifying. In practice, the least bit of interference would leave the passenger an idiot or a good imitation of a corpse. Over interplanetary distances you'd have to worry not only about intervening dust and gas, but about red and violet shifts due to gravity and relative velocities. And what happens to your soul?

I worry about that. I don't necessarily believe in a soul; I don't believe in taking chances. If my soul isn't recorded somewhere in the process, I'm dead, even though my memory remains as reconstructed electron tracks.

Where society is concerned, there are equally serious problems.

Let's say we've reached step one. We've recorded our customer and we now have a record and a ball of ionised plasma. Why not beam the record to two receivers? Now we've got a duplicator. The legalities get sticky. We could get around them by permitting one, say, one Isaac Asimov to a planet; but who gets the royalties on the FOUNDATION trilogy?

Similarly, you can keep the record. You fire the signal at the receiver, but you store the tape. Ten years later the passenger walks in front of a bus. You can recreate him from tape, minus ten years of his life. But—aside from questions concerning his soul—can he collect his own life insurance?

Suppose we change our mind after step one. We store the tape instead of firing it. Is it kidnapping? Or, in view of the fact that we have mortally vaporized a man, is it murder? Does it cease to be murder if we reconstitute him before the trial?

Finally, we assume an advance whereby we needn't destroy the model to get the record. Shouldn't we destroy him anyway? Otherwise he hasn't *gone* anywhere.

Our fourth method doesn't have these difficulties. It is often called tranposition or teletransposition, but that's too much work. Henceforth I'll call it teleportation. It involves making two points in space contiguous . . . somehow. Generally we take advantage of the fact that the universe, as viewed from four or more dimensions, resembles a crumpled handkerchief. Light follows the contours of the handkerchief, so that spaces which are really contiguous in four or more dimensions do not look contiguous when viewed across apparently flat space.

If the universe does not in fact resemble a crumpled handkerchief, maybe we can *make* it resemble a crumpled handkerchief. It may be possible to bend the fabric of space by the judicious application of electromagnetic fields, until two points touch. At least we get no embarrassing duplication of passengers.

The embarrassment arises if two sets of machines are in operation at once, *anywhere in the universe*. At best, space will be bent in some unanticipated way, and nobody will get where he wants to go. At worst, the fabric of space comes apart like a too-often crumpled handkerchief.

DEVELOPMENT OF MECHANICAL TELEPORTATION: Assume we have a teleportation transmitter and receiver. How we got these is a matter for science fiction; but once we have them we can move onto surer ground. We assume that the principle does not involve beaming; it may involve tunnel diode effects or space-bending or something new.

So we've got two enclosed booths . . .
Why booths?

Because of an old principle that two bodies cannot occupy the same space at the same time. Like a lot of old principles, this one isn't strictly true. Matter is mostly empty space. There is no reason why you can't teleport into a rock; there's plenty of room for your atoms and the rock's atoms. Trouble is, it'll kill you.

Teleporting into a mass of air will kill you too. There are energy factors involved, and also bends, embolisms, etc. Probably there will be an explosion.

So you need booths. Naturally the interior spaces are identical in size and shape. The transmitter booth includes air as well as the passenger or cargo. The receiver is evacuated. We teleport the air as well as the passenger and/or cargo.

If what we have are transceivers, we need not evacuate the receiver. We teleport its air to the transmitter as we teleport the cargo to the receiver.

With development, we may be able to do away with the booths. If we expand a spherical force field from a point (GREE stories, from Galaxy) to get a vacuum for the receiver, we need only a transmitter booth. Put the passenger in a pressure suit and we eliminate that booth; it doesn't matter how big a volume gets sent along as long as the volume of the receiver is bigger.

But we'll have to start with booths.

Now turn to Figure 1 (page 92).

Booths A and B are used for the first stages of experiment, to find out if we can teleport reliably.

Once they are working well we move to step II: teleporting instruments from booth C to B and (if transceivers) back again. If conservation of energy holds, we expect a rise in temperature from teleporting down that cliff.

Booth D is built on railroad tracks. We set it moving to determine if conservation of momentum holds. Given relativity, we might as well use booth D as receiver only. Thus we can pad the back wall, in case conservation does hold.

Booths E and F test for continuous teleportation.

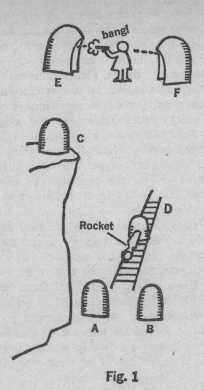

Fig. 1

Bullets are fired into the opening in E at various speeds. Which bullet will reach F before it strikes the back wall of E? This system could stand redesigning. Obviously we can't pad the back wall of E; we'd only teleport the padding to F. Thus we destroy a teleport booth every time the bullet hits the back wall of E. When the bullet teleports in time, it zings out of booth F and hits the scientist. If the scientist ducks, the coward, the bullet will still destroy booth E.

We can get better data with a long crossbow bolt, by measuring what length of the bolt gets teleported in time. But we destroy the booth with the arrowhead and clonk the scientist with the feathered end. I'm *sure* there's a better way to design this system.

PRACTICE OF MECHANICAL TELEPORTATION: Here my theme becomes complex. I intend to demonstrate that any limitations we assume for our teleportation system are going to imply a society: one society for each set of limitations. Again, I will quote my sources where I can remember them, sometimes. But much of what follows is my own.

I

THE ASSUMPTION: We don't need a transmitter. Our teleport receiver will bring anything to itself, from anywhere. Limitations may exist as to distance or mass of cargo.

THE RESULT: Thieves capable of stealing anything from anyone in perfect safety. Such machinery was discovered by Seaton, and later by DuQuesne, in THE SKYLARK OF SPACE. In practice, anyone who has such machinery is king of the world. If many men have transmitterless receivers, society falls apart. When society stops making parts for the machines, the machines fall apart, and everything starts over.

II

THE ASSUMPTION: No receiver is needed. Our teleport transmitter will place its cargo anywhere we choose.

THE RESULT: We can put a bomb anywhere. The idea was used at least once, in THE PERSON FROM PORLOCK. In practice, a government that owned one of these would—again—own the world. Two such governments would probably bomb each other back to a pre-teleport level of civilization. Presumably it could happen any number of times.

III

Given the assumptions in (I) and (II) you don't really get a society. You get a short war. Hence most stories assume that teleportation requires both a transmitter and a receiver.

Let's do the same. Let us further assume that transmitters (transceivers?) look like telephone booths. You walk into a booth, you put a coin in the slot, you dial. You're elsewhere.

How do they work? We assume either space-bending or the tunnel diode effect. We assume the operation is relatively cheap: no more than a few quarters in the slot. Finally, a slug in the slot will send the customer straight to police headquarters.

THE RESULT: All present transportation becomes obsolete: cars and trucks and freeways, ships and docks, airliners and airports, trains and train stations. What do we do with a continental net of freeways once the cars and busses have disappeared? You use them for drag races and bicycle riding; you put houses on them or turn them into parks. Or you pack them with cars because there's no place else to put the damn useless cars. Not only freeways and turnpikes, but streets and roads and even sidewalks become obsolete. In business districts you keep the sidewalks for window shopping. Elsewhere, pffttt!

The mind boggles. Assume the population problem continues in the direction it's going. Then, as Isaac Asimov has suggested, new generations could grow up without seeing the exterior of *any* building, including their own homes. There might soon be no countryside to see in any case, and precious few exteriors to buildings. Without need for streets or sidewalks, there would be no space between buildings; they would be built wall to wall, or in units a mile cubic. And the people get their exercise by riding bicycles between two open booths arranged like E and F in Figure I.

IV

But suppose there are limitations on the booths? For each assumed limitation one gets a different society. Let's take a few examples.

THE ASSUMPTION: Booths are expensive to operate. The price for any jump, regardless of distance, is two hundred dollars. (A reasonable restriction. Any space-stressing operation might well cost as much as any other. Ditto for a single tunnel-diode operation.)

THE RESULT: Cars, motor scooters, busses will remain. Except for emergencies, nobody would use booths for distances shorter than a transcontinental flight. But airplanes would disappear, except perhaps for cargo flights.

Change the price and you change the result. As price goes down, freight traffic by train and truck dwindles, and then even automobiles begin to go. Raise the price to a few thousand dollars, and only spacecraft disappear.

THE ASSUMPTION: The booths are cheap, a couple of bucks a jump, but limited as to distance. Ten miles, let us say, is the upper limit.

THE RESULT: A traveler would move in "hops", naturally. But there would come a point where an airplane is cheaper or more convenient, or both, than a succession of teleport booths. Thus, cars would go, but airplanes and shipping would remain.

Change the limiting distance and, again, you change the society. At a mile a jump only the cars go. At a thousand miles a jump, only spacecraft remain.

THE ASSUMPTION: Teleportation is limited by the Laws of Conservation of Energy and Momentum.

THE RESULT: Not very different from above. Cars would go, airplanes would remain. By teleportation we could not travel long distance north and south; we would have to do it on short hops. The longer the hop, the harder momentum would jerk the passenger sideways each time.

Traveling east, our momentum would lift us a few inches from the chair of the receiver booth on each hop. (Yes, I said chair. *You* might try it standing up, but I wouldn't.) Traveling west would be worse: momentum would slam you down hard. A New Yorker might prefer to reach San Francisco via the western route, in a line of booths crossing the Atlantic and Pacific Oceans.*

Notice one important exception. We can travel from the northern hemisphere to the southern in perfect comfort, provided the departure point and destination are at corresponding latitudes.

Elevators become more important than ever. In Earth's gravitational field, at ground level, we lose seven degrees Fahrenheit for every mile we teleport upward . . . and we gain as much going downhill. Elevators are more comfortable.

So: you want to go skiing in the Swiss Alps, at St. Moritz. From the United States your best bet is to take a plane to someplace with a big landing field, ride an elevator half a mile up to a teleportation booth, then teleport to St. Moritz. Do it any other way and you wind up sick for a couple of days. But from New York you can reach Angol, Chile in one jump!

---

* Assume a passenger is at the equator, teleporting straight east a distance of X miles.

Then X/4000 is the angle $ of his jump in *radians*. For X small, we take sine$ = $ and get $\frac{X \times 1000}{4000} = \frac{X}{4}$. [We multiplied the sine of the angle, equal to the angle itself for small angles given in radians, by the rotational velocity of the Earth.] X/4 is the velocity at which the passenger gets lifted off his feet.

Going west, he gets slammed *down,* same equation.

For small angles, the equation holds elsewhere than at the equator. Decreasing the distance from the Earth's axis of rotation decreases the speed of rotation, but *increases* the angle of shift.

V

So much for booths. They still look like our best attempt at prophecy; but let's try some wilder ideas and see what we get.

THE ASSUMPTION: Open teleport discs. You step on a disc, it teleports you to another disc. Cost, pennies per thousand trips.

THE RESULTS: All present transportation disappears. With the proper setup, you can *walk* anywhere on the planet. Figure 2 is a design for intercity trans-

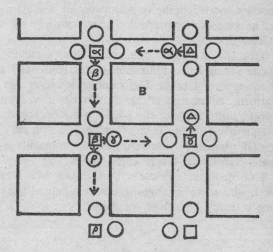

Layout of stepping discs in
a rectilinear city. Shown
is a walk around the block B:

α,β,γ,Δ,α.
To go straight, one merely
maintains a normal walking
pace, as in β thru ρ
Dotted arrows = teleportation.

Fig. 2

portation, but it can easily be adapted for longer distances. The blocks shown could be lines of longitude and latitude; their length is optional.

For the rectangular city layout shown, we simply walk in the direction we wish to go. The distance between the receiver plate, at the center of the intersection, and the next transmitter disc is about three paces. In three paces one covers a block, whose length, I repeat, is optional. Perhaps there would be faster lanes through the center of town, and faster still between towns: intersections a mile or ten miles apart. To get out of the system one walks *around* the final disc and goes window shopping or whatever.

The biggest advantage is that we can give up all the endless dialling!

THE ASSUMPTION: Our transmitter is hand sized. We can hang it from our belt. It has (oh, well) a telephone-type dial on it. The receiver is bigger: an open platform, either a small plate at home, in vestibule, or a community receiver the size of a public square. Cost is equivalent to the cost of using a telephone. There are (if necessary) compensators for momentum—and heat—transfer in the receiver plates.

THE RESULT: Bester's THE STARS MY DESTINATION, with minor changes. No mazes behind the doors; simply unlisted receiver numbers.

VI

Shall we design a few spacecraft? Limited teleportation might not make spacecraft obsolete. It might even be used to improve the spacecraft themselves.

THE ASSUMPTIONS: Teleportation requires both a transmitter and a receiver. Conservation holds. Teleportation is instantaneous, and does not involve beaming.

THE RESULT: See Figure 3. The ship consists mainly of a couple of rocket motors, fuel tanks, and an

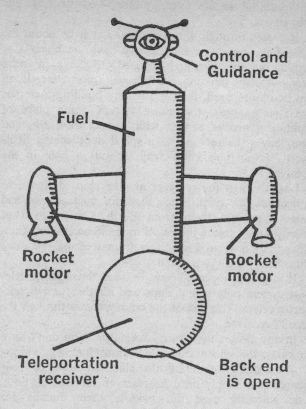

Control and Guidance

Fuel

Rocket motor

Rocket motor

Teleportation receiver

Back end is open

Fig. 3

open-ended teleportation receiver open to the rear. You can leave it open because, in vacuum, you don't need to worry about air getting in the receiver.

The ship, unmanned, is fired from Earth orbit or from further out. Probably it should be fired in the direction of the galactic core, where we anticipate more traffic. By firing the ship from, say, Jupiter orbit, we can pack quite a lot of fuel—water, for reaction mass—*outside* the ship. (See Isaac Asimov, THE MARTIAN WAY.)

We use all the fuel except a reserve for steering. The ship coasts.

It passes through a star system. Let it be about the size of the solar system; then we have ten hours (assuming our ship is near lightspeed) to shove an entire prefab colony into the Earth-based transmitter. If all ten hours are used, then the colony building materials are strewn across the entire system. Each piece of equipment arrives at rest with respect to Earth, and thus leaves the receiver at a speed approaching lightspeed. (Now you know why we put a hole in the receiver.)

Last through the receiver are the ships designed to collect all this crap. Since they are manned, we had better not send them from Earth. Conservation of energy would freeze the pilots to ice in an instant. Consider the irony: to keep them from freezing, we must ship them from Pluto orbit!

It might be more efficient to send through the teleport system only a few ships and another prefab teleport receiver. The rest of the colony comes through the second receiver.

In any case, notice four advantages. You don't have to carry the entire cargo, or waste fuel accelerating it. You don't decelerate the ship, so none of your limited fuel supply need be reserved for that purpose. The colonists need not twiddle their thumbs for decades. And the ship can be re-used.

Can and will. You just let it coast. Every time it comes near a star system, you have another colony. In eighty thousand years we leave a line of colonies clear across the galaxy, before we finally run out of stars.

Less peaceful societies would shove war fleets through the teleport system. It is hard to imagine a safer way to make war. The fleet is strewn all across the system, with all the warships at rest with respect to the universe at large. And how could the target system counterattack? To reach the invading system, they would have to catch a ship which has had years to accelerate to its tremendous velocity, and which is long gone into interstellar space before the attack can even begin.

During the Boston speech, a member of the audience suggested that teleportation be used to fuel the above craft. Specifically: the motor is a receiver, open, with a flared nozzle attached. We drop a transmitter on Jupiter. Presto! Hellishly dense high-pressure gas expands explosively into the vacuum of space, driving the ship forward. Fuel supply: inefficient compared to ion drives or the like, but almost literally unlimited.

It won't work. Rather, it won't work for long.

Remember, we have assumed that conservation holds. The motor's exhaust velocity is the ship's own limiting velocity if we use teleportation to fuel the ship. Jupiter's atmosphere wouldn't expand fast enough to be useful. Even with a fusion drive, we lose momentum every time a droplet of hydrogen reaches the fuel tank. We have to get it back by firing the droplet through the rocket motor. When the two velocities balance . . . we can't go any faster.

Total conversion of matter to light does give us unlimited velocity. Then we have only the problem of what to do with the incoming fuel. We *always* have that problem. A droplet of hydrogen moving at a tenth of lightspeed would vaporize any fuel tank we can build today. Maybe in the future . . . with new materials . . . plenty of padding . . . springs . . .

Let's try something else.

THE ASSUMPTIONS: The distance one can teleport is relatively restricted. The greater the curvature of space—that is, the greater the proximity to a large mass—the shorter is the limiting distance.

We will assume that on Earth the limiting distance is two feet; around Mars's orbit, some miles; between stars, a few light minutes. Attempt to send a mass beyond the limiting distance, and it will emerge from the receiver as a fluid or a fine dust. The curvature of space distorts the relationships between atoms too greatly.

Again, we assume the conservation laws hold.

THE RESULTS: Feeble as far as true teleportation is concerned. We can teleport fluids, so fuel tanks disappear except for storage tanks and spacecraft. The best we can do for spacecraft is fuel a booster, with a heavily armored fuel tank, designed to lift spacecraft out of a gravity well at low speed. But we can use the system to build a ship . . .

See Figure 4 (page 103). We'll call this peculiar object the "end-teleport drive," and we'll say that it teleports itself onto its own front end. I invented it many years ago, but I never had the nerve to write a story about it.

Notice that if you push the button, the ship teleports onto its own front end; but if you hold the button down, it will teleport repeatedly, in a steady stream of images. One jump brings the ship to position 2; but the moment it begins to occupy position 2 it wants to be at position 3; as that image starts to form the ship wants to be at position 4, et cetera. If teleportation is rapid enough we can use it for transportation.

You refuse to believe in my ship? Then think of it as an exercise in speculation. Ridiculous as it may seem, we do get results.

1) Rate-of-travel of the ship is limited only by mechanical difficulties, that is, by the rate of successive teleportation. The end-teleport drive does not affect the ship's kinetic energy. We change only the position. So there is none of this nonsense about relativity.

2) We *must* assume a mechanical limit on rate-of-travel. Otherwise the ship goes off the edge of the universe.

3) You can take your finger off the button. Kinetic

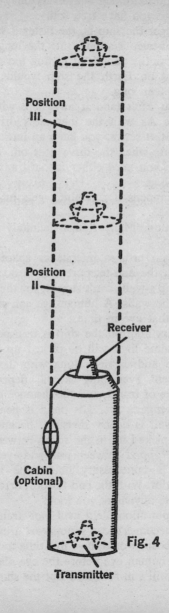

Position
III

Position
II

Receiver

Cabin
(optional)

Fig. 4

Transmitter

energy is teleported along with everything else; and as a perfect image you have free will.

4) The longer the ship is, the faster it will go, with a given rate-of-teleportation. But: the longer the ship is, the greater is the danger of getting too near a large mass. To land on Earth the ship would have to be less than two feet long.

In fact, you can't land it anywhere with the end-teleport drive. As with the inertialess drives in Doc Smith's LENSMAN series, you keep an intrinsic velocity which reappears when the drive goes off. To land the ship anywhere you need either inboard auxiliary rockets, or rocket tugs.

5) What happens if something gets in the way of the ship?

Good question. Many things definitely will. Light, for example.

A light beam crosses interstellar space. Suddenly, for an instant, the end-teleport ship is occupying that space. The ship's walls can't stop it, for the light never encountered the walls. A human eye can stop it if the light reaches that eye in time.

Result: everything on the ship is transparent. If we assume that some light will be picked up by the teleportation field and carried along with the ship, then how transparent everything is will depend on two things: the rate of travel, and the distance of an object from the passenger's eye. His hand is nearly opaque. The further wall is nearly invisible, because so much light is being picked up in the space between wall and eye . . . and *dropped* between wall and eye. The cabin in Figure 4 is unnecessary unless the ship carries rocket auxiliaries. With the end-teleport drive going, the stars are visible anywhere you look.

If the teleportation field will *not* transport light, the situation becomes more serious. At a useful rate of travel a light beam would have just time to traverse the diameter of a human eye before the eye disappears. So a human eye will still function. But the ship and all its contents, including the passenger, are totally invisible, and each passenger becomes a disembodied viewpoint falling between the stars.

Travel even faster, and a light beam may have time to touch the retina without first entering the lens of the eye. Now everything becomes a blur. On arrival the passenger becomes a psychiatric patient.

6) Interstellar dust would also be picked up en route. Most of it could be handled by a tough air conditioning system; but a certain proportion would appear already inside the transitory space occupied by the passenger. Definitely he would need medical attention on arrival.

7) Interstellar hydrogen would be swept up by the moving ship. Aboard an end-teleport drive there would be absolutely no smoking. Drinking, yes . . .

8) As for meteors and larger bodies . . . we'll use a trick.

Let's say we're going toward the galactic core, i. e. toward Sagitarius. Okay. Before we leave the system, we take our ship to within a few million miles of the Sun, on the Sagitarius side; and we hover.

We hover by end-teleporting outward as the Sun's gravity draws us inward. Half an hour of this should give us a respectable intrinsic velocity Sunward. *Now* we take off toward Sagitarius.

So we ram someting en route. It can happen.

But . . . it takes energy to make two solid masses occupy the same space. Chances are we *cannot* teleport *into* what we've rammed. A fuse blows and the motor stops. That leaves the ship with its intrinsic velocity, which we have built up hugely in a direction opposite to the direction of travel.

So the ship backs up at hundreds of miles per second! Even if we ram a *planet,* our intrinsic velocity is higher than escape velocity, and we're safe.

9) Conservation of energy rears its head once more. The ship becomes fiendishly cold as it leaves the solar system, and body temperature drops simultaneously.

The reverse occurs as we enter a system. It's a good thing we built a heavy air conditioning system to get rid of all that dust. We'll need it for temperature control.

VII

Why do I persist in assuming that the conservation laws hold?

This question caused a series of soapbox speeches, mostly in my defense (thanks, friends), along the back wall of my Boston audience. The assumptions are important, and I'm going to try to justify them.

1) The behavior of the universe does not change. In all known cases the laws of conservation of energy and momentum hold rigorously. Now we use them for prediction. The existence and most of the properties of the neutrino were predicted by use of these and other conservation laws. Later the neutrino itself was detected through judicious use of its own proposed properties.

If today's physicists can use conservation to predict ghost particles, I can use them to predict the behavior of a teleport system.

2) In any case, I'm entitled to make any assumptions I like, if they are internally consistent. This is an exercise in speculation, remember? Speculation starts with assumptions. If you don't like mine, try your own; you might get some interesting results.

3) A passenger teleporting downhill must lose potential energy. Some equivalent gain in energy must appear. But why heat?

Good question. I myself generally assume that the energy will appear as a jump in electron orbits. Then the electrons drop back, releasing photons. The photons are absorbed before they reach the passenger's skin, giving heat. But almost any reasonable process will ultimately end in heat. Heat is the most general, most randomized form of energy.

Could the released energy appear as neutrinos? That

would *not* give heat. But it would upset some of the obscure parity laws of nuclear physics (thus upsetting Isaac Asimov, Hal Clement, and thousands of reactionary physicists), and it would make uphill teleportation impossible, for the process would have to destroy neutrinos which weren't there in the first place.

VIII

How about a perpetual motion machine?

See Figure 5 (page 107). The idea is to use open transmitter and receiver booths. The cargo, thirty gal-

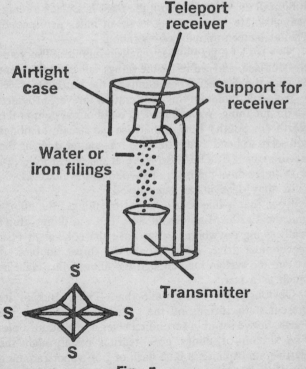

Teleport receiver

Airtight case

Support for receiver

Water or iron filings

Transmitter

Fig. 5

lons of water, is teleported to the receiver. It immediately pours out into the open transmitter, which teleports it back to the receiver, et cetera. Put a water wheel in the system and we get power.

Obviously there's a flaw. If conservation holds, the water freezes pretty quick. Furthermore, thermodynamics says that the energy to run the system will be greater than the maximum energy to be obtained from the continuously falling water.

But the system is interesting in other ways.

Let's replace the water with a ton of iron filings. That way we can enclose the whole system in a vacuum chamber and stop worrying about atmospheric friction, water evaporation, and freezing of the water. We let the filings fall under gravity until the mass is a black stream, near absolute zero, moving at seven miles per second. That's nineteen minutes of operation.

Now we let it go another nineteen minutes. The velocity doubles, and we've let the filings fall the equivalent of twice the distance from infinity to the Earth's surface.

We could maintain this acceleration forever, provided we do one thing. We will have to build our system at the North (or South) Pole. Otherwise the stream of filings will seem to bend away from the transmitter door as the Earth turns. (BOOM!) So we're at the North Pole . . .

In thirty days the mass of the filings has doubled.

In sixty days it has quadrupled.

Note that while Earth pulls the filings, the filings pull the Earth. Minutely, at first. But the filings aren't really going anywhere, so we have the equivalent of a reactionless drive. Every month the thrust doubles. If we run the system long enough the filings will weight as much as a star.

Obviously we don't want that. Tides! But in its present state, turning off the system would destroy the Earth. So we set up a second receiver at the South Pole. The stream of filings goes tearing off through the Earth's atmosphere, a blue flash of iron vapor ramming air. Even the gamma rays are going upward! What a

show! Listen to that applause! But all the teevee
cameras have melted. . .

Well, this is where I quit. But try a few postulates
yourself, and see what you get.

THE THEORY AND PRACTICE
OF TIME TRAVEL

Speculate: (2) To ponder a subject in its different aspects and relations; meditate; esp. to theorise from conjectures without sufficient evidence.
—*Webster's New Collegiate Dictionary, 1959*

Once upon a time a man was given three wishes. He blew the first two, getting himself in such deep trouble that if he let either wish stand, he would suffer terribly. Now desperate, he cried, "I wish I'd never *had* a fairy godmother!" And the past healed to cancel both wishes.

The first time-travel story was a fairy tale—here drastically condensed.

Its theme is buried deep in the literature. L. Frank Baum used it in THE WONDERFUL LAND OF OZ. Cabell borrowed it for THE SILVER STALLION. Traditionally the protagonist may change the past without actually moving backward in time.

H. G. Wells, one of the fathers of modern science fiction, also fathered the time traveling *vehicle*. This may be the reason Well's spiritual sons tend to treat time travel as science fiction rather than fantasy. But Wells wrote only of travel into the future. He missed the Grandfather Paradox and all the other derivative paradoxes of travel into the past. His time machine was a mere vehicle, no more remarkable than the gravity-shielding material, Cavorite.*

* Both were mere philosophical vehicles. Wells liked to preach.

Wells also missed the most important aspect of time travel: wish fulfillment. When a child prays, "Please, God, make it didn't happen," he is inventing time travel in its essence. (He will probably give up the idea when he learns good English. More about that later.) The prime purpose of time travel is to change the past; and the prime danger is that the Traveler might change the past. The man who first thought of travel into the past combined the Wells machine with the fairy tale to produce time travel in its present form.

Time machines come in many forms. Well's man-carrying vehicle was as open as a bicycle seat, with a magnificent view of time flashing past. Poul Anderson's standard issue time Patrol vehicle could do anything Well's could, and fly too.

More restricted machines may travel only into the future, or may send only subatomic particles into the past, or may be restricted to things even less substantial: thoughts, dreams, emotional states. Others may move only in quantum jumps of a million or sixty million years. A writer who puts severe limits on his time machine, is generally limiting its ability to change the past in order to make his story less incredible.

THE GRANDFATHER PARADOX is basic to any discussion of time travel. It runs as follows:

At the age of eighty your grandfather invents a time machine. You hate the old man, so you steal the machine and take it sixty years back into the past and kill him. How can they suspect you?

But you've killed him before he can meet your grandmother. Thus you were never born. He didn't get a chance to build the time machine either.

But then you can't have killed him. Thus he may sire your father, who may sire you. Later there will be a time machine. . .

You and the machine both do and do not exist. Paradox!

In general we will call any such interference with

the past, especially self-cancelling interference, a Grand-father Paradox.

Travel into the past violates certain of what we regard as laws of nature.

(1) A vehicle which travels from the thirtieth century AD to the twentieth, may be regarded as appearing from nowhere. Thus it violates the law of conservation of matter. If the vehicle carries a power source of any kind, it also violates conservation of energy . . . a quibble, as they are both the same law these days.

To say that an equivalent tonnage of matter disappears a thousand years later is no answer. For ten centuries there was an extra time machine around.

But things are even worse if a Grandfather Paradox is involved. One can imagine a centuries-old time machine resting in a museum, inside a glass-and-steel case made from the glass and the steel which would have been used to build the time machine, if anyone had gone ahead and built that time machine, which nobody did, because of interference with the past via that same time machine.

(2) If one cannot send matter through time, perhaps one can send signals—information.

But even this violates conservation of energy. Any signal involves energy in some form.

Furthermore, relativity laws state that information cannot travel faster than c, the velocity of light in a vacuum. A signal traveling back through time travels faster than infinity!

(3) Physical time travel clearly violates any law of motion, as motion always relates to time. This affects conservation of momentum, statements about kinetic energy, and even the law of gravity. *Anybody's* law of gravity.

(4) What about drawing information from the future?

If precognition and prophecy are only very accurate

guesswork by the subconscious mind, then no laws are violated. But if precognition really has something to do with time—

I cite the Heisenberg Principle. One cannot observe something without affecting it. If one observes the future, there must be an energy exchange of some kind. But that implies that the future one is observing is *the* future; that it already exists; that information is flowing into the past.

I've demonstrated that this violates relativity and conservation of energy. It also involves a Grandfather Paradox, if information drawn from one future is used to create another. And if the information can't be used to change the future, then what good is it?

What was that about the stock market?

(5) Travel into the future is no more difficult than suspended animation and a good, durable time capsule. But you can't go home without traveling into the past.

Does any of this seem like nitpicking? Sure it is. Are we to regard the laws of relativity and conservation as sacred, never to be broken, nor even bent by exceptions? Heaven forbid.

But time travel violates laws more basic than conservation laws.

Our belief in laws of any kind presupposes a belief in cause and effect. Time travel reverses cause and effect. With a Grandfather Paradox operating, the effect, coming before the cause, may cause the cause never to come into effect, with results which are not even self-consistent.

Characters in time-travel stories often complain that English isn't really built to handle time travel. The tenses get all fouled up. We in the trade call this problem Excedrin Headache number $\sqrt{-3.14159}$ . . .

To show it in action, I'd like to quote from one of my own stories, BIRD IN THE HAND. The characters have done catastrophic damage to the past, and are discussing how to repair it.

"Maybe we can go around you." Svetz hesitated, then plunged in. "Zeera, try this. Send me back to an hour before the earlier Zeera arrives. Ford's automobile won't have disappeared yet. I'll duplicate it, duplicate the duplicate, take the reversed duplicate and the original past you in the big extension cage. That leaves you to destroy the duplicate instead of the original. I reappear after you've gone, leave the original automobile for Ford, and come back here with the reversed duplicate. How's that?"

"It sounded great. Would you mind going through it again?"

"Let's see. I go back to—"

This was less of a digression than it seemed. The English language can't handle time travel. We conclude that the ancestors who made our language didn't have minds equipped to handle time travel. Naturally we don't either; for our thinking is too dependent on our language.

As far as I know, *no* language has tenses equipped to handle time travel. No language on Earth. Yet.

But then, no language was ever equipped to handle lasers, television, or spaceflight until lasers, television, and spaceflight were developed. Then the words followed.

If time travel were thrust upon us, would we develop a language to handle it?

We'd need a basic past tense, an altered past tense, a potential past tense (might have been), an altered future tense, an excised future tense (for a future that can no longer happen), a home base present tense, a present-of-the-moment tense, an enclosed present tense (for use while the vehicle is moving through time), a future past tense ("I'll meet you at the bombing of Pearl

Harbor in half an hour."), a past future tense ("Just a souvenir I picked up ten million years from now"), and many more. We'd need at least two directions of time flow: sequential personal time, and universal time, with a complete set of tenses for each.

We'd need pronouns to distinguish [you of the past] from [you of the future] and [you of the present]. After all, the three of you might all be sitting around the same table someday.

Meanwhile (if, God willing, the word still has meaning), time travel must be considered fantasy. It violates too many of the laws of physics and reason to be thought otherwise.

But it's a form of fantasy superbly suited to games of logic. The temptation to work out a self-consistent set of laws for time travel must be enormous. So many writers have tried it!

Let's look at some of the more popular possibilities:

DEFENSE OF TIME TRAVEL #1: Assume that (1) One can travel *only* into the future. (2) The universe is cyclic in time, repeating itself over and over.

This works! All you've got to do is go into the future past the Big Collapse when the universe falls in on itself, through the Big Bang when it explodes again, and keep going until you reach the area of the past you're looking for. Then you murder Hitler in 1920, or use the H-bomb on the damyankees at Appomatox, or whatever your daydream is. There is no Grandfather Paradox. You merely get a new future.

True, the next version of *you* will not make the trip. You've eliminated his motive. Thus on the *next* cycle the damyankees *will* win the Civil War, Hitler *will* lead Germany into WWII, and so forth. But you've merely introduced a double cycle. There is no paradox.

Further, your time machine need be nothing more than an EXTREMELY durable time capsule.

OBJECTIONS: Three. First, some people don't believe in cyclic time. (I don't.) Second, locating the proper era is a nontrivial problem when you've got the whole lifetime of the universe to search in. You'd be lucky to find *any* section of human history. Third, removing your time capsule from the reaction of the Big Bang could change the final configuration of matter, giving an entirely different history.

DEFENSE OF TIME TRAVEL #II: Known as the theory of multiple time tracks.

Let there be a myriad of realities, of universes. For every decision made by any form of life, let it be made both ways; or in all possible ways if there are more then two choices. Let universes be created with every choice.

Then conservation of matter and energy holds only for the universe of universes. One can move time machines from one universe to another.

You've got to admit it's flamboyant!

You still can't visit the past. But you can find a universe where things happened more slowly; where Napoleon is *about* to fight Waterloo, or Nero is *about* to ascend the throne. Or, instead of changing the past, you need only seek out the universe where the past you want is the one that happened. The universe you want unquestionably exists. (Though you may search a long, weary time before you find it.)

Ersatz time travel becomes a special case of sidewise-in-time travel, travel between multiple time tracks.

The *what-if* story has fascinated many writers. Even O. Henry wrote at least one. From our viewpoint, sidewise-in-time travel solves conservation laws, Grandfather Paradox, everything.

I *hate* sidewise-in-time travel stories.

Let me show you why.

First, they're too easy to write. You don't need a brain to write alternate-world stories. You need a good history text.

In the second place . . . did you ever sweat over a

decision? Think about one that really gave you trouble, because you knew that what you did would affect you for the rest of your life. Now imagine that for every way you could have jumped, one of you in one universe did jump that way.

Now don't you feel silly? Sweating over something so trivial, when you were going to take *all* the choices anyway. And if you think that's silly, consider that one of you still can't decide. . .

In the third place, probability doesn't support the theory of alternate time tracks.

There are six ways a die can fall, right? Which makes thirty-six ways that *two* dice can fall, including six ways to get a seven. Each way the dice can fall determines one universe. Then the chance of your ending in each of the thirty-six universes is one in thirty-six, right?

Then it doesn't matter if the dice are loaded. One chance in thirty-six, exactly, is the odds for each way the dice can fall. One chance in six, exactly, of getting a seven.

Experience, however, shows that it *does* matter if the dice are loaded.

DEFENSE OE TIME TRAVEL #III: The idea of reversing the flow of time isn't nearly as silly as it sounds. I quote from an article in the October 1969 issue of *Scientific American,* "EXPERIMENTS IN TIME REVERSAL," by Oliver E. Overseth.

"All of us vividly recognise the way time flows; we take considerable comfort, for example, in our confidence that the carefully arranged marriage of gin and vermouth is not going to be suddenly annulled in our glass, leaving us with two layers of warm liquid and a lump of ice. It is a curious fact, however, that the laws that provide the basis for our understanding of fundamental physical processes (and presumably biological processes as well) do not favor one direction of time's arrow over another. They would represent the world just as well if time were flowing backward instead of forward and martinis were coming apart rather than being created."

Is the universe really invarient under time reversal? Many physicists think not. Overseth and his partner Roth spent almost two years looking for a case in subatomic physics in which invarience under time reversal is not preserved.

They knew exactly what they were looking for. They were watching (via some very indirect instruments) the decay of a lambda particle into a proton plus a pi meson. The anomaly would have been a nonzero value for the beta component of the spin of the proton.

The point is that they failed to find what they were looking for. There have been many such experiments in recent years, and none have been successful. At the subatomic level, one cannot tell whether time is running backward or forward.

Could a determined man reach the past by reversing himself in time and waiting for last year to happen again?

Present theory says that he would reverse both the spin and the charge of every subatomic particle in his body. The charge reversal converts the whole mass to antimatter. BOOM!

Less dramatically, there is conservation of mass/ energy. Reverse the direction of travel in time of a human body, and to any physicist it would look like two people have vanished.

Clearly this is illegal. We can't do it that way.

We might more successfully reverse a man's *viewpoint*: send his *mind* backward in time. If there is really no difference between past and future, except in attitude, then it should be possible.

But the traveler risks his memory healing to a *tabula rasa*, a blank slate. When he reaches his target date he might not remember what to do about it.

For there is still entropy: the tendency to disorder in the universe, and the most obvious effect of moving "forward" in time. Entropy is not obvious where few reactions are involved, as in the motion of the planets, or as when a lambda particle breaks down. But the mushroom cloud left by a hydrogen bomb is difficult to return to its metal case. That's entropy.

Any specialist in geriatric medicine knows about entropy.

Let's try something less ambitious.

Suppose we found a clump of particles already moving backward in time. (Exactly what Roth and Overseth and their brethren might find in their experiments, if time-reversal turns out to be valid. Though most expect to find just the opposite.) Now we write messages on that clump. Simple messages. "Blue Ben in the sixth, 4/4/72."

But from our viewpoint, we start by finding a message and end by erasing it! And if it went wrong. . . We find a message: "Blue Ben in the sixth, 4/4/72." We bet on him, and he loses. Now what? Can we unwrite a different message? Or just refuse to erase it at all?

But if it did work, we could make a fortune. And it violates no known physical laws! Practically.

Meanwhile, Roth and Overseth and a number of others are all convinced that there must be exceptions to the symmetry of time. If they find just one, it's all over.

DEFENSE OF TIME TRAVEL #IV: The oldest of all, going back to Greek times. Philosophers call it *fatalism* or *determinism*. A fatalist believes that everything that happens is predetermined to the end of time; that any attempt to change the predetermined future is fated, is a part of the predetermined future itself.

To a fatalist, the future looks exactly like the traditional picture of the past. Both are rigid, inflexible. The introduction of time travel would not alter the picture at all, for any attempt on the part of a time traveler to change the past has already been made, and is a part of the past.

Fatalism has been the basis for many a tale of a frantic time traveler caught in a web of circumstance such that every move he makes acts to bring about just the calamity he is trying to avert. The standard plot sketch is reminiscent of *Oedipus Rex*; when well done it has the same flavor of man heroically battling Fate—and losing.

Notice how fatalism solves the Grandfather Paradox. You can't kill your grandfather, because you *didn't*. You'll kill the wrong man if you try it; or your gun won't fire.

Fatalism ruins the wish-fulfillment aspect of time travel. Anything that averts the Grandfather Paradox will do that. The Grandfather Paradox *is* the wish-fulfillment aspect. *Make it didn't happen*.

The way to get the most fun out of time travel is to accept it for what it is. Give up relativity and the conservation laws. Allow changes in the past and present and future, reversals in the order of cause and effect, effects whose cause never happens. . .

Fatalistic time travel also allows these causative loops, but they are always simple, closed loops with no missing parts. The appearance of a time machine somewhere always implies its disappearance somewhere-and-somewhen else. But with this new, *free will* kind of time travel. . .

We assume that there is only one reality, one past and one future; but that it can be changed at will via the time machine. Cause and effect may loop toward the past; and sometimes a loop is pinched off, to vanish from the time stream. The traveler who kills his six-year-old grandfather eliminates the cause of *himself*, but he and his time machine remain—until someone else changes the past even further back.

Between the deterministic and free will modes of time travel lies a kind of compromise position:

We assume a kind of inertia, or hysteresis effect, or

special conservation law for time travel. The past resists change. Breaks in time tend to heal. Kill Charlemagne and someone will take his place, conquer his empire, mate with his wives, breed sons very like his. Changes will be minor and local.

Fritz Leiber used Conservation of Events to good effect in the Change War stories. In TRY AND CHANGE THE PAST, his protagonist went to enormous lengths to prevent a bullet from smashing through a man's head. He was sincere. It was his own head. In the end he succeeded—and watched a bullet-sized meteorite smash into his alter-self's forehead.

Probabilities change to protect history. This is the safest form of time travel in that respect. But one does have to remember that the odds have changed.

Try to save Jesus with a submachine gun, and the gun will *positively* jam.

But if you did succeed in killing your own six-year-old grandfather, you would stand a good chance of taking his place. Conservation of Events requires someone to take his place; and everyone else is busy filling his own role. Except *you,* an extraneous figure from another time. Now Conservation of Events acts to protect you in your new role!

Besides, you're already carrying the old man's genes. . . .

Certain kinds of time travel may be possible; but changing the past is not. I can prove it.

GIVEN: That the universe of discourse permits both time travel and the changing of the past.

THEN: A time machine will not be invented in that universe.

For, if a time machine is invented in that universe, somebody will change the past of that universe. There is just too much future subsequent to the invention of a time machine: too many people with too many good motives for meddling with too many events occurring in too much of the past.

If we assume that there is no historical inertia, no Conservation of Events, then each change makes a whole new universe. Every trip into the past means that all the dice have to be thrown over again. Every least change changes all the history books, until by chance and endless change we reach a universe where there is no time machine invented, ever, by any species.

Then that universe would not change.

Now assume that there *is* an inertia to history; that the past tends to remain unchanged; that probabilities change to protect the fabric of events. What is the simplest change in history that will protect the past from interference?

Right. No time machines!

NIVEN'S LAW: IF THE UNIVERSE OF DISCOURSE PERMITS THE POSSIBILITY OF TIME TRAVEL AND OF CHANGING THE PAST, THEN NO TIME MACHINE WILL BE INVENTED IN THAT UNIVERSE.

If time travel is so manifestly impossible, why does every good and bad science fiction writer want to write a new, fresh time travel story?

It's a form of competition. No writer believes that a field is completely mined out. And no field ever is. There is always something new to say, if you can find it.

Time travel can be a vehicle, like a faster-than-light drive. Our best evidence says that nothing can travel faster than light. Yet hard-headed science fiction writers constantly use faster-than-light spacecraft. If a character must reach the Veil Nebula, and if the plot demands that his girl friend be still a girl when he returns, then he must needs travel faster than light. Similarly, it takes time travel to pit a man against a dinosaur, or to match a modern man against King Arthur's knights.

There are things a writer can't say without using time travel.

Then, time travel is so delightfully open to tortuous reasoning. You should be convinced of that by now.

The brain gets needed exercise plotting a story in a universe where effects happen before their causes; where the hero and his enemy may be working each to prevent the other's birth; where a brick wall may be no more solid than a dream, if one can eliminate the architect from history.

If one could travel in time, what wish could not be answered? All the treasures of the past would fall to one man with a submachine gun. Cleopatra and Helen of Troy might share his bed, if bribed with a trunkful of modern cosmetics. The dead return to life, or cease to have been at all.

Bothered by smog? Henry Ford could be stopped in time, in time. . .

No. We face insecurity enough. Read your newspaper, and be glad that at least your past is safe.

INCONSTANT MOON

I

I was watching the news when the change came, like a flicker of motion at the corner of my eye. I turned toward the balcony window. Whatever it was, I was too late to catch it.

The moon was very bright tonight.

I saw that, and smiled, and turned back. Johnny Carson was just starting his monologue.

When the first commercials came on I got up to re-heat some coffee. Commercials came in strings of three and four, going on midnight. I'd have time.

The moonlight caught me coming back. If it had been bright before, it was brighter now. Hypnotic. I opened the sliding glass door and stepped out onto the balcony.

The balcony wasn't much more than a railed ledge, with standing room for a man and a woman and a portable barbecue set. These past months the view had been lovely, especially around sunset. The Power and Light Company had been putting up a glass-slab style office building. So far it was only a steel framework of open girders. Shadow-blackened against a red sunset sky, it tended to look stark and surrealistic and hellishly impressive.

Tonight. . .

I had never seen the moon so bright, not even in the desert. *Bright enough to read by,* I thought, and immediately, *but that's an illusion.* The moon was never

124

bigger (I had read somewhere) than a quarter held nine feet away. It couldn't possibly be bright enough to read by.

It was only three-quarters full!

But, glowing high over the San Diego Freeway to the west, the moon seemed to dim even the streaming automobile headlights. I blinked against its light, and thought of men walking on the moon, leaving corrugated footprints. Once, for the sake of an article I was writing, I had been allowed to pick up a bone-dry moon rock and hold it in my hand. . . .

I heard the show starting again, and I stepped inside. But, glancing once behind me, I caught the moon growing even brighter—as if it had come from behind a wisp of scudding cloud.

Now its light was brain-searing, lunatic.

The phone rang five times before she answered.

"Hi," I said. "Listen—"

"Hi," Leslie said sleepily, complainingly. Damn. I'd hoped she was watching television, like me.

I said, "Don't scream and shout, because I had a reason for calling. You're in bed, right? Get up and—can you get up?"

"What time is it?"

"Quarter of twelve."

"Oh, Lord."

"Go out on your balcony and look around."

"Okay."

The phone clunked. I waited. Leslie's balcony faced north and west, like mine, but it was ten stories higher, with a correspondingly better view.

Through my own window, the moon burned like a textured spotlight.

"Stan? You there?"

"Yah. What do you think of it?"

"It's gorgeous. I've never seen anything like it. What could make the moon light up like that?"

"I don't know, but isn't it gorgeous?"

"You're supposed to be the native." Leslie had only moved out here a year ago.

"Listen, I've *never* seen it like this. But there's an old legend," I said. "Once every hundred years the Los Angeles smog rolls away for a single night, leaving the air as clear as interstellar space. That way the gods can see if Los Angeles is still there. If it is, they roll the smog back so they won't have to look at it."

"I used to know all that stuff. Well, listen, I'm glad you woke me up to see it, but I've got to get to work tomorrow."

"Poor baby."

"That's life. 'Night."

" 'Night."

Afterward I sat in the dark, trying to think of someone else to call. Call a girl at midnight, invite her to step outside and look at the moonlight . . . and she may think it's romantic or she may be furious, but she won't assume you called six others.

So I thought of some names. But the girls who belonged to them had all dropped away over the past year or so, after I started spending all my time with Leslie. One could hardly blame them. And now Joan was in Texas and Hildy was getting married, and if I called Louise I'd probably get Gordie too. The English girl? But I couldn't remember her number. Or her last name.

Besides, everyone I knew punched a time clock of one kind or another. Me, I worked for a living, but as a freelance writer I picked my hours. Anyone I woke up tonight, I'd be ruining her morning. Ah, well. . .

The Johnny Carson Show was a swirl of grey and a roar of static when I got back to the living room. I turned the set off and went back out on the balcony.

The moon was brighter than the flow of headlights on the freeway, brighter than Westwood Village off to the right. The Santa Monica Mountains had a magical pearly glow. There were no stars near the moon. Stars could not survive that glare.

I wrote science and how-to articles for a living. I ought to be able to figure out what was making the moon do that. Could the moon be suddenly larger? . . . Inflating like a balloon? No. Closer, maybe. The moon, falling?

Tides! Waves fifty feet high . . . and earthquakes! San Andreas Fault splitting apart like the Grand Canyon! Jump in my car, head for the hills . . . no, too late already. . .

Nonsense. The moon was brighter, not bigger. I could see that. And what could possibly drop the moon on our heads like that?

I blinked, and the moon left an afterimage on my retinae. It was *that* bright.

A million people must be watching the moon right now, and wondering, like me. An article on the subject would sell big . . . if I wrote it before anyone else did. . .

There must be some simple, obvious explanation.

Well, how could the moon grow brighter? Moonlight was reflected sunlight. Could the sun have gotten brighter? It must have happened after sunset, then, or it would have been noticed. . . .

I didn't like that idea.

Besides, half the Earth was in direct sunlight. A thousand correspondents for Life and Time and Newsweek and Associated Press would all be calling in from Europe, Asia, Africa . . . unless they were all hiding in cellars. Or dead. Or voiceless, because the sun was blanketing everything with static, radio and phone systems and television . . . television. Oh my God.

I was just barely beginning to be afraid.

All right, start over. The moon had become very much brighter. Moonlight, well, moonlight was reflected sunlight; any idiot knew that. Then . . . something had happened to the sun.

II

"Hello?"

"Hi. Me," I said, and then my throat froze solid. Panic! What was I going to *tell* her?

"I've been watching the moon," she said dreamily. "It's wonderful. I even tried to use my telescope, but I couldn't see a thing; it was too bright. It lights up the whole city. The hills are all silver."

That's right, she kept a telescope on her balcony. I'd forgotten.

"I haven't tried to go back to sleep," she said. "Too much light."

I got my throat working again. "Listen, Leslie love, I started thinking about how I woke you up and how you probably couldn't get back to sleep, what with all this light. So let's go out for a midnight snack."

"Are you out of your mind?"

"No, I'm serious. I mean it. Tonight isn't a night for sleeping. We may never have a night like this again. To hell with your diet. Let's celebrate. Hot fudge sundaes, Irish Coffee—"

"That's different. I'll get dressed."

"I'll be right over."

Leslie lived on the fourteenth floor of Building C of the Barrington Plaza. I rapped for admission, and waited.

And waiting, I wondered without any sense of urgency: Why Leslie?

There must be other ways to spend my last night on Earth, than with one particular girl. I could have picked a different particular girl, or even several not too particular girls, except that that didn't really apply to me, did it? Or I could have called my brother, or either set of parents—

Well, but brother Mike would have wanted a good

reason for being hauled out of bed at midnight. "But, Mike, the moon is so beautiful—" Hardly. Any of my parents would have reacted similarly. Well, I had a good reason, but would they believe me?

And if they did, what then? I would have arranged a kind of wake. Let 'em sleep through it. What I wanted was someone who would join my . . . farewell party without asking the wrong questions.

What I wanted was Leslie. I knocked again.

She opened the door just a crack for me. She was in her underwear. A stiff, misshapen girdle in one hand brushed my back as she came into my arms. "I was about to put this on."

"I came just in time, then." I took the girdle away from her and dropped it. I stooped to get my arms under her ribs, straightened up with effort, and walked us to the bedroom with her feet dangling against my ankles.

Her skin was cold. She must have been outside.

"So!" she demanded. "You think you can compete with a hot fudge sundae, do you?"

"Certainly. My pride demands it." We were both somewhat out of breath. Once in our lives I had tried to lift her cradled in my arms, in conventional movie style. I'd damn near broken my back. Leslie was a big girl, my height, and almost too heavy around the hips.

I dropped us on the bed, side by side. I reached around her from both sides to scratch her back, knowing it would leave her helpless to resist me, *ah* ha hahahaha. She made sounds of pleasure to tell me where to scratch. She pulled my shirt up around my shoulders and began scratching my back.

We pulled pieces of clothing from ourselves and each other, at random, dropping them over the edges of the bed. Leslie's skin was warm now, almost hot . . .

All right, now *that's* why I couldn't have picked another girl. I'd have to teach her how to scratch. And there just wasn't time.

Some nights I had a nervous tendency to hurry our lovemaking. Tonight we were performing a ritual, a rite of passage. I tried to slow it down, to make it last. I tried to make Leslie like it more. It paid off incredibly. I forgot the moon and the future when Leslie put her heels against the backs of my knees and we moved into the ancient rhythm.

But the image that came to me at the climax was vivid and frightening. We were in a ring of blue-hot fire that closed like a noose. If I moaned in terror and ecstasy, then she must have thought it was ecstasy alone.

We lay side by side, drowsy, torpid, clinging together. I was minded to go back to sleep then, renege on my promise, sleep and let Leslie sleep . . . but instead I whispered into her ear: "Hot fudge sundae." She smiled and stirred and presently rolled off the bed.

I wouldn't let her wear the girdle. "It's past midnight. Nobody's going to pick you up, because I'd thrash the blackguard, right? So why not be comfortable?" She laughed and gave in. We hugged each other once, hard, in the elevator. It felt much better without the girdle.

III

The grey-haired counter waitress was cheerful and excited. Her eyes glowed. She spoke as if confiding a secret. "Have you noticed the moonlight?"

Ships's was fairly crowded, this time of night and this close to UCLA. Half the customers were university students. Tonight they talked in hushed voices, turning to look out through the glass walls of the twenty-four-hour restaurant. The moon was low in the west, low enough to compete with the street globes.

"We noticed," I said. "We're celebrating. Get us two hot fudge sundaes, will you?" When she turned her back I slid a ten dollar bill under the paper place mat. Not that she'd ever spend it, but at least she'd have the pleasure of finding it. I'd never spend it either.

I felt loose, casual. A lot of problems seemed suddenly to have solved themselves.

Who would have believed that peace could come to Vietnam and Cambodia in a single night?

This thing had started around eleven thirty, here in California. That would have put the noon sun just over the Arabian Sea, with all but a few fringes of Asia, Europe, Africa, and Australia in direct sunlight.

Already Germany was reunited, the Wall melted or smashed by shock waves. Israelis and Arabs had laid down their arms. Apartheid was dead in Africa.

And I was free. For me there were no more consequences. Tonight I could satisfy all my dark urges, rob, kill, cheat on my income tax, throw bricks at plate glass windows, burn my credit cards. I could forget the article on explosive metal forming, due Thursday. Tonight I could substitute cinnamon candy for Leslie's Pills. Tonight—

"Think I'll have a cigarette."

Leslie looked at me oddly. "I thought you'd given that up."

"You remember. I told myself if I got any overpowering urges, I'd have a cigarette. I did that because I couldn't stand the thought of never smoking again."

"But it's been months!" she laughed.

"But they keep putting cigarette ads in my magazines!"

"It's a plot. All right, go have a cigarette."

I put coins in the machine, hesitated over the choice, finally picked a mild filter. It wasn't that I wanted a cigarette. But certain events call for champagne, and others for cigarettes. There is the traditional last cigarette before a firing squad . . .

I lit up. *Here's to lung cancer.*

It tasted just as good as I remembered; though there was a faint stale undertaste, like a mouthful of old cigarette butts. The third lungful hit me oddly. My eyes unfocused and everything went very calm. My heart pulsed loudly in my throat.

"How does it taste?"

"Strange. I'm buzzed," I said.

Buzzed! I hadn't even heard the word in fifteen years. In high school we'd smoked to get that buzz, that quasi-drunkenness produced by capillaries constricting in the brain. The buzz had stopped coming after the first few times, but we'd kept smoking, most of us . . .

I put it out. The waitress was picking up our sundaes.

Hot and cold, sweet and bitter: there is no taste quite like that of a hot fudge sundae. To die without tasting it again would have been a crying shame. But with Leslie it was a *thing,* a symbol of all rich living. Watching her eat was more fun than eating myself.

Besides . . . I'd killed the cigarette to taste the ice cream. Now, instead of savoring the ice cream, I was anticipating Irish coffee.

Too little time.

Leslie's dish was empty. She stage-whispered, "Aahh!" and patted herself over the navel.

A customer at one of the small tables began to go mad.

I'd noticed him coming in. A lean scholarly type wearing sideburns and steel-rimmed glasses, he had been continually twisting around to look out at the moon. Like others at other tables, he seemed high on a rare and lovely natural phenomenon.

Then he got it. I saw his face changing, showing suspicion, then disbelief, then horror, horror and helplessness.

"Let's go," I told Leslie. I dropped quarters on the counter and stood up.

"Don't you want to finish yours?"

"Nope. We've got things to do. How about some Irish coffee?"

"And a Pink Lady for me? Oh, look!" She turned full around.

The scholar was climbing up on a table. He balanced, spread wide his arms and bellowed, "Look out your windows!"

"You get down from there!" a waitress demanded, jerking emphatically at his pants leg.

"The world is coming to an end! Far away on the other side of the sea, death and hellfire—"

But we were out the door, laughing as we ran. Leslie panted, "We may have—escaped a religious—riot in there!"

I thought of the ten I'd left under my plate. Now it would please nobody. Inside, a prophet was shouting his message of doom to all who would hear. The grey-haired woman with the glowing eyes would find the money and think: They knew it too.

Buildings blocked the moon from the Red Barn's parking lot. The street lights and the indirect moonglare were pretty much the same color. The night only seemed a bit brighter than usual.

I didn't understand why Leslie stopped suddenly in the driveway. But I followed her gaze, straight up to where a star burned very brightly just south of the zenith.

"Pretty," I said.

She gave me a very odd look.

There were no windows in the Red Barn. Dim artificial lighting, far dimmer than the queer cold light outside, showed on dark wood and quietly cheerful customers. Nobody seemed aware that tonight was different from other nights.

The sparse Tuesday night crowd was gathered mostly around the piano bar. A customer had the mike. He was singing some half-familiar song in a wavering weak voice, while the black pianist grinned and played a schmaltzy background.

I ordered two Irish coffees and a Pink Lady. At Leslie's questioning look I only smiled mysteriously.

How ordinary the Red Barn felt. How relaxed; how happy. We held hands across the table, and I smiled and was afraid to speak. If I broke the spell, if I said the wrong thing . . .

The drinks arrived. I raised an Irish coffee glass by the stem. Sugar, Irish whiskey, and strong black coffee, with thick whipped cream floating on top. It coursed through me like a magical potion of strength, dark and hot and powerful.

The waitress waved back my money. "See that man in the turtleneck, there at the end of the piano bar? He's buying," she said with relish. "He came in two hours ago and handed the bartender a hundred dollar bill."

So that was where all the happiness was coming from. Free drinks! I looked over, wondering what the guy was celebrating.

A thick-necked, wide-shouldered man in a turtleneck and sports coat, he sat hunched over into himself, with a wide bar glass clutched tight in one hand. The pianist offered him the mike, and he waved it by, the gesture giving me a good look at his face. A square, strong face, now drunk and miserable and scared. He was ready to cry from fear.

So I knew what he was celebrating.

Leslie made a face. "They didn't make the Pink Lady right."

There's one bar in the world that makes a Pink Lady the way Leslie likes it, and it isn't in Los Angeles. I passed her the other Irish coffee, grinning an I-told-you-so grin. Forcing it. The other man's fear was contagious. She smiled back, lifted her glass and said, "To the blue moonlight."

I lifted my glass to her, and drank. But it wasn't the toast I would have chosen.

The man in the turtleneck slid down from his stool. He moved carefully toward the door, his course slow and straight as an ocean liner cruising into dock. He pulled the door wide, and turned around, holding it open, so that the weird blue-white light streamed past his broad black silhouette.

Bastard. He was waiting for someone to figure it out, to shout out the truth to the rest. *Fire and doom—*

"Shut the door!" someone bellowed.

"Time to go," I said softly.

"What's the hurry?"

The hurry? He might *speak!* But I couldn't say that . . .

Leslie put her hand over mine. "I know. I *know.* But we can't run away from it, can we?"

A fist closed hard on my heart. She'd known, and I hadn't noticed?

The door closed, leaving the Red Barn in reddish dusk. The man who had been buying drinks was gone.

"Oh, God. When did you figure it out?"

"Before you came over," she said. "But when I tried to check it out, it didn't work."

"Check it out?"

"I went out on the balcony and turned the telescope on Jupiter. Mars is below the horizon these nights. If the sun's gone nova, all the planets ought to be lit up like the moon, right?"

"Right. Damn." I should have thought of that myself. But Leslie was the stargazer. I knew some astrophysics, but I couldn't have found Jupiter to save my life.

"But Jupiter wasn't any brighter than usual. So then I didn't know *what* to think."

"But then—" I felt hope dawning fiery hot. Then I remembered. "That star, just overhead. The one you stared at."

"Jupiter."

"All lit up like a fucking neon sign. Well, that tears it."

"Keep your voice down."

I *had* been keeping my voice down. But for a wild moment I wanted to stand up on a table and scream! *Fire and doom*—What right had they to be ignorant?

Leslie's hand closed tight on mine. The urge passed. It left me shuddering. "Let's get out of here. Let 'em think there's going to be a dawn."

"There is." Leslie laughed a bitter, barking laugh like nothing I'd ever heard from her. She walked out while I was reaching for my wallet—and remembering that there was no need.

Poor Leslie. Finding Jupiter its normal self must have looked like a reprieve—until the white spark flared to shining glory an hour and a half late. An hour and a half, for sunlight to reach Earth by way of Jupiter.

When I reached the door Leslie was half-running down Westwood toward Santa Monica. I cursed and ran to catch up, wondering if she'd suddenly gone crazy.

Then I noticed the shadows ahead of us. All along the other side of Santa Monica Boulevard: moon shadows, in horizontal patterns of dark and blue-white bands.

I caught her at the corner.

The moon was setting.

A setting moon always looks tremendous. Tonight it glared at us through the gap of sky beneath the freeway, terribly bright, casting an incredible complexity of lines and shadows. Even the unlighted crescent glowed pearly bright with earthshine.

Which told me all I wanted to know about what was happening on the lighted side of Earth.

And on the moon? The men of Apollo Nineteen must have died in the first few minutes of nova sunlight. Trapped out on a lunar plain, hiding perhaps behind a melting boulder . . . Or were they on the night side? I couldn't remember. Hell, they could outlive us all. I felt a stab of envy and hatred.

And pride. We'd put them there. We reached the moon before the nova came. A little longer, we'd have reached the stars.

The disc changed oddly as it set. A dome, a flying saucer, a lens, a line . . .

Gone.

Gone. Well, that was that. Now we could forget it; now we could walk around outside without being constantly reminded that something was *wrong*. Moon-set had taken all the queer shadows out of the city.

But the clouds had an odd glow to them. As clouds glow after sunset, tonight the clouds shone livid white at their western edges. And they streamed too quickly across the sky. As if they tried to run . . .

When I turned to Leslie, there were big tears rolling down her cheeks.

"Oh, damn." I took her arm. "Now stop it. Stop it."

"I can't. You know I can't stop crying once I get started."

"This wasn't what I had in mind. I thought we'd do things we've been putting off, things we like. It's our last chance. Is this the way you want to die, crying on a street corner?"

"I don't want to die at all!"

"Tough shit!"

"Thanks a lot." Her face was all red and twisted. Leslie was crying as a baby cries, without regard for dignity or appearance. I felt awful. I felt guilty, and I *knew* the nova wasn't my fault, and it made me angry.

"I don't want to die either!" I snarled at her. "You show me a way out and I'll take it. Where would we go? The South Pole? It'd just take longer. The moon must be molten all across its day side. Mars? When this is over Mars will be part of the sun, like the Earth. Alpha Centauri? The acceleration we'd need, we'd be spread across a wall like peanut butter and jelly—"

"Oh, shut up."

"Right."

"Hawaii. Stan, we could get to the airport in twenty minutes. We'd get two hours extra, going west! Two hours more before sunrise!"

She had something there. Two hours was worth any price! But I'd worked this out before, staring at the moon from my balcony. "No. We'd die sooner. Listen, love, we saw the moon go bright about midnight. That means California was at the back of the Earth when the sun went nova."

"Yes, that's right."

"Then we must be furthest from the shock wave."

She blinked. "I don't understand."

"Look at it this way. First the sun explodes. That heats the air and the oceans, all in a flash, all across the day side. The steam and superheated air expand *fast*. A flaming shock wave comes roaring over into the night side. It's closing on us right now. Like a noose. But it'll reach Hawaii first. Hawaii is two hours closer to the sunset line."

"Then we won't see the dawn. We won't live even that long."

"No."

"You explain things so well," she said bitterly. "A flaming shock wave. So graphic."

"Sorry. I've been thinking about it too much. Wondering what it will be like."

"Well, stop it." She came to me and put her face in my shoulder. She cried quietly. I held her with one arm and used the other to rub her neck, and I watched the streaming clouds, and I didn't think about what it would be like.

Didn't think about the ring of fire closing on us.

It was the wrong picture anyway.

I thought of how the oceans had boiled on the day side, so that the shock wave had been mostly steam to start with. I thought of the millions of square miles of ocean it had to cross. It would be cooler and wetter when it reached us. And the Earth's rotation would spin it like the whirlpool in a bathtub.

Two counterrotating hurricanes of live steam, one north, one south. That was how it would come. We were lucky. California would be near the eye of the northern one.

A hurricane wind of live steam. It would pick a man up and cook him in the air, strip the steamed flesh from him and cast him aside. It was going to hurt like hell.

We would never see the sunrise. In a way that was a pity. It would be spectacular.

Thick parallel streamers of clouds were drifting

across the stars, too fast, their bellies white by city light. Jupiter dimmed, then went out. Could it be starting already? Heat lightning jumped—

"Aurora," I said.

"What?"

"There's a shock wave from the sun, too. There should be an aurora like nothing anybody's ever seen before."

Leslie laughed suddenly, jarringly. "It seems so strange, standing on a street corner talking like this! Stan, are we dreaming it?"

"We could pretend—"

"No. Most of the human race must be dead already."

"Yah."

"And there's nowhere to go."

"Damn it, you figured that out long ago, all by yourself. Why bring it up now?"

"You could have let me sleep," she said bitterly. "I was dropping off to sleep when you whispered in my ear."

I didn't answer. It was true.

" 'Hot fudge sundae'," she quoted. Then, "It wasn't a bad idea, actually. Breaking my diet."

I started to giggle.

"Stop that."

"We could go back to your place now. Or my place. To sleep."

"I suppose. But we couldn't sleep, could we? No, don't say it. We take sleeping pills, and five hours from now we wake up screaming. I'd rather stay awake. At least we'll know what's happening."

But if we took all the pills . . . but I didn't say it. I said, "Then how about a picnic?"

"Where?"

"The beach, maybe. Who cares? We can decide later."

IV

All the markets were closed. But the liquor store next to the Red Barn was one I'd been using for years. They sold us foie gras, crackers, a couple of bottles of chilled champagne, six kinds of cheese and a hell of a lot of nuts—I took one of everything—more crackers, a bag of ice, frozen rumaki hors d'oeuvres, a fifth of an ancient brandy that cost twenty-five bucks, a matching fifth of Cherry Heering for Leslie, six-packs of beer and Bitter Orange . . .

By the time we had piled all that into a dinky store cart, it was raining. Big fat drops spattered in flurries across the acre of plate glass that fronted the store. Wind howled around the corners.

The salesman was in a fey mood, bursting with energy. He'd been watching the moon all night. "And now this!" he exclaimed as he packed our loot into bags. He was a small, muscular old man with thick arms and shoulders. "It *never* rains like this in California. It comes down straight and heavy, when it comes at all. Takes days to build up."

"I know." I wrote him a check, feeling guilty about it. He'd known me long enough to trust me. But the check was good. There were funds to cover it. Before opening hours the check would be ash, and all the banks in the world would be bubbling in the heat of the sun. But that was hardly my fault.

He piled our bags in the cart, set himself at the door. "Now when the rain lets up, we'll run these out. Ready?" I got ready to open the door. The rain came like someone had thrown a bucket of water at the window. In a moment it had stopped, though water still streamed down the glass. "Now!" cried the salesman, and I threw the door open and we were off. We reached the car laughing like maniacs. The wind howled around us, sweeping up spray and hurling it at us.

"We picked a good break. You know what this weather reminds me of? Kansas," said the salesman. "During a tornado."

Then suddenly the sky was full of gravel! We yelped and ducked, and the car rang to a million tiny concussions, and I got the car door unlocked and pulled Leslie and the salesman in after me. We rubbed our bruised heads and looked out at white gravel bouncing everywhere.

The salesman picked a small white pebble out of his collar. He put it in Leslie's hand, and she gave a startled squeak and handed it to me, and it was cold.

"Hail," said the salesman. "Now I really don't get it."

Neither did I. I could only think that it had something to do with the nova. But what? How?

"I've got to get back," said the salesman. The hail had expended itself in one brief flurry. He braced himself, then went out of the car like a marine taking a hill. We never saw him again.

The clouds were churning up there, forming and disappearing, sliding past each other faster than I'd ever seen clouds move; their bellies glowing by city light.

"It must be the nova," Leslie said shivering.

"But how? If the shock wave were here already, we'd be *dead*—or at least deaf. Hail?"

"Who cares? Stan, we don't have *time!*"

I shook myself. "All right. What would you like to do most, right now?"

"Watch a baseball game."

"It's two in the morning," I pointed out.

"That lets out a lot of things, doesn't it?"

"Right. We've hopped our last bar. We've seen our last play, and our last clean movie. What's left?"

"Looking in jewelry store windows."

"Seriously? Your last night on Earth?"

She considered, then answered. "Yes."

By damn, she meant it. I couldn't think of anything duller. "Westwood or Beverly Hills?"

"Both."

"Now, *look*—"

"Beverly Hills, then."

We drove through another spatter of rain and hail—
a capsule tempest. We parked half a block from the Tiffany salesroom.

The sidewalk was one continuous puddle. Second-
hand rain dripped on us from various levels of the
buildings overhead. Leslie said, "This is great. There
must be half a dozen jewelry stores in walking distance."

"I was thinking of driving."

"No no no, you don't have the proper attitude. One
must window shop on foot. It's in the rules."

"But the rain!"

"You won't die of pneumonia. You won't have time,"
she said, too grimly.

Tiffany's had a small branch office in Beverly Hills,
but they didn't put expensive things in the windows at
night. There were a few fascinating toys, that was all.

We turned up Rodeo Drive—and struck it rich.
Tibor showed an infinite selection of rings, ornate and
modern, large and small, in all kinds of precious and
semiprecious stones. Across the street, Van Cleef and
Arpel showed brooches, men's wristwatches of elegant
design, bracelets with tiny watches in them, and one
window that was all diamonds.

"Oh, lovely," Leslie breathed, caught by the flashing
diamonds. "What they must look like in daylight! . . .
Wups—"

"No, that's a good thought. Imagine them at dawn,
flaming with nova light, while the windows shatter to
let the raw daylight in. Want one? The necklace?"

"Oh, *May* I? Hey, hey, I was kidding! Put that down,
you idiot, there must be alarms in the glass."

"Look, nobody's going to be wearing any of that stuff
between now and morning. Why shouldn't we get some
good out of it?"

"We'd be caught!"

"Well, you *said* you wanted to window shop . . ."

"I don't want to spend my last hour in a cell. If you'd brought the car we'd have *some* chance—"

"—Of getting away. Right. I *wanted* to bring the car—" But at that point we both cracked up entirely, and had to stagger away holding onto each other for balance.

There were a good half dozen jewelry stores on Rodeo. But there was more. Toys, books, shirts and ties in odd and advanced styling. In Francis Orr, a huge plastic cube full of new pennies. A couple of damn strange clocks further on. There was an extra kick in window shopping, knowing that we could break a window and take anything we wanted badly enough.

We walked hand in hand, swinging our arms. The sidewalks were ours alone; all others had fled the mad weather. The clouds still churned overhead.

"I wish I'd known it was coming," Leslie said suddenly. "I spent the whole day fixing a mistake in a program. Now we'll never run it."

"What would you have done with the time? A baseball game?"

"Maybe. No. The standings don't matter now." She frowned at dresses in a store window. "What would you have done?"

"Gone to the Blue Sphere for cocktails," I said promptly. "It's a topless place. I used to go there all the time. I hear they've gone full nude now."

"I've never been to one of those. How late are they open?"

"Forget it. It's almost two-thirty."

Leslie mused, looking at giant stuffed animals in a toy store window. "Isn't there someone you would have murdered, if you'd had the time?"

"Now, you *know* my agent lives in New York."

"Why him?"

"My child, why would any writer want to murder his agent? For the manuscripts he loses under other manuscripts. For his ill-gotten ten percent, and the remaining ninety percent that he sends me grudgingly and late. For—"

Suddenly the wind roared and rose up against us. Leslie pointed, and we ran for a deep doorway that turned out to be Gucchi's. We huddled against the glass.

The wind was suddenly choked with hail the size of marbles. Glass broke somewhere, and alarms lifted thin, frail voices into the wind. There was more than hail in the wind! There were rocks!

I caught the smell and taste of seawater.

We clung together in the expensively wasted space in front of Gucchi's. I coined a short-lived phrase and screamed, "Nova weather! How the blazes did it—" But I couldn't hear myself, and Leslie didn't even know I was shouting.

Nova weather. How did it get here so fast? Coming over the pole, the nova shock wave would have to travel about four thousand miles—at least a five hour trip.

No. The shock wave would travel in the stratosphere, where the speed of sound was higher, then propagate down. Three hours was plenty of time. Still, I thought, it should not have come as a rising wind. On the other side of the world, the exploding sun was tearing our atmosphere away and hurling it at the stars. The shock should have come as a single vast thunderclap.

For an instant the wind gentled, and I ran down the sidewalk pulling Leslie after me. We found another doorway as the wind picked up again. I thought I heard a siren coming to answer the alarm.

At the next break we splashed across Wilshire and reached the car. We sat there panting, waiting for the heater to warm up. My shoes felt squishy. The wet clothes struck to my skin.

Leslie shouted, "How much longer?"

"I don't know! We ought to have *some* time."

"We'll have to spend our picnic indoors!"

"Your place or mine? Yours," I decided, and pulled away from the curb.

V

Wilshire Boulevard was flooded to the hubcaps in spots. The spurt of hail and sleet had become a steady, pounding rain. Fog lay flat and waist deep ahead of us, broke swirling over our hood, churned in a wake behind us. Weird weather.

Nova weather. The shock wave of scalding super-heated steam hadn't happened. Instead, a mere hot wind roaring through the stratosphere, the turbulence eddying down to form strange storms at ground level.

We parked illegally on the upper parking level. My one glimpse of the lower level showed it to be flooded. I opened the trunk and lifted two heavy paper bags.

"We must have been crazy," Leslie said, shaking her head. "We'll never use all this."

"Let's take it up anyway."

She laughed at me. "But why?"

"Just a whim. Will you help me carry it?"

We took double armfuls up to the fourteenth floor. That still left a couple of bags in the trunk. "Never mind them," Leslie said. "We've got the rumaki and the bottles and the nuts. What more do we need?"

"The cheeses. The crackers. The foie gras."

"Forget 'em."

"No."

"You're out of your mind," she explained to me, slowly so that I would understand. "You could be steamed dead on the way down! We might not have more than a few minutes left, and you want food for a week! *Why?*"

"I'd rather not say."

"Go then!" She slammed the door with terrible force.

The elevator was an ordeal. I kept wondering if Leslie was right. The shrilling of the wind was muffled, here at the core of the building. Perhaps it was about to rip electrical cables somwhere, leave me stranded in a darkened box. But I made it down.

The upper level was knee deep in water.

My second surprise was that it was lukewarm, like old bathwater, unpleasant to wade through. Steam curdled on the surface, then blew away on a wind that howled through the concrete echo chamber like the screaming of the damned.

Going up was another ordeal. If what I was thinking was wish fulfillment, if a roaring wind of live steam caught me now . . . I'd feel like such an idiot. . . . But the doors opened, and the lights hadn't even flickered.

Leslie wouldn't let me in.

"Go away!" She shouted through the locked door. "Go eat your cheese and crackers somewhere else!"

"You got another date?"

That was a mistake. I got no answer at all.

I could almost see her viewpoint. The extra trip for the extra bags was no big thing to fight about; but why did it have to be? How long was our love affair going to last, anyway? An hour, with luck. Why back down on a perfectly good argument, to preserve so ephemeral a thing?

"I wasn't going to bring this up," I shouted, hoping she could hear me through the door. The wind must be three times as loud on the other side. "We may need food for a week! And a place to hide!"

Silence. I began to wonder if I could kick the door down. Would I be better off waiting in the hall? Eventually she'd have to—

The door opened. Leslie was pale. "That was cruel," she said quietly.

"I can't promise anything. I wanted to wait, but you forced it. I've been wondering if the sun really has exploded."

"That's cruel. I was just getting used to the idea."
She turned her face to the door jamb. Tired, she was
tired. I'd kept her up too late. . . .

"Listen to me. It was all wrong," I said. "There
should have been an aurora borealis to light up the
night sky from pole to pole. A shock wave of particles
exploding out of the sun, traveling at an inch short of
the speed of light, would rip into the atmosphere like—
why, we'd have seen blue fire over every building!

"Then, the storm came too slow," I screamed, to be
heard above the thunder. "A nova would rip away the
sky over half the planet. The shock wave would move
around the night side with a sound to break all the
glass in the world, all at once! And crack concrete and
marble—and, Leslie love, it just hasn't happened. So
I started wondering."

She said it in a mumble. "Then what is it?"

"A flare. The worst—"

She shouted it at me like an accusation. "A flare! A
solar flare! You think the sun could light up like
that—"

"Easy, now—"

"—could turn the moon and planets into so many
torches, then fade out as if nothing had happened!
Oh, you idiot—"

"May I come in?"

She looked surprised. She stepped aside, and I bent
and picked up the bags and walked in.

The glass doors rattled as if giants were trying to
beat their way in. Rain had squeezed through cracks
to make dark puddles on the rug.

I set the bags on the kitchen counter. I found bread
in the refrigerator, dropped two slices in the toaster.
While they were toasting I opened the foie gras.

"My telescope's gone," she said. Sure enough, it
was. The tripod was all by itself on the balcony, on its
side.

I untwisted the wire on a champagne bottle. The
toast popped up, and Leslie found a knife and spread

both slices with foie gras. I held the bottle near her ear, figuring to trip conditioned reflexes.

She did smile fleetingly as the cork popped. She said, "We should set up our picnic grounds here. Behind the counter. Sooner or later the wind is going to break those doors and shower glass all over everything."

That was a good thought. I slid around the partition, swept all the pillows off the floor and the couch and came back with them. We set up a nest for ourselves.

It was kind of cosy. The kitchen counter was three and a half feet high, just over our heads, and the kitchen alcove itself was just wide enough to swing our elbows comfortably. Now the floor was all pillows. Leslie poured the champagne into brandy snifters, all the way to the lip.

I searched for a toast, but there were just too many possibilities, all depressing. We drank without toasting. And then carefully set the snifters down and slid forward into each other's arms. We could sit that way, face to face, leaning sideways against each other.

"We're going to die," she said.

"Maybe not."

"Get used to the idea, I have," she said. "Look at you, you're all nervous now. Afraid of dying. Hasn't it been a lovely night?"

"Unique. I wish I'd known in time to take you to dinner."

Thunder came in a string of six explosions. Like bombs in an air raid. "Me too," she said when we could hear again.

"I wish I'd known this afternoon."

"Pecan pralines!"

"Farmer's Market. Double-roasted peanuts. Who would *you* have murdered, if you'd had the time?"

"There was a girl in my sorority—"

—and she was guilty of sibling rivalry, so Leslie claimed. I named an editor who kept changing his mind. Leslie named one of my old girl friends, I named her only old boy friend that I knew about, and it got to be kind of fun before we ran out. My brother Mike had forgotten my birthday once. The fiend.

The lights flickered, then came on again.

Too casually, Leslie asked, "Do you really think the sun might go back to normal?"

"It better *be* back to normal. Otherwise we're dead anyway. I wish we could see Jupiter."

"Dammit, answer me! Do you think it was a flare?"

"Yes."

"Why?"

"Yellow dwarf stars don't go nova."

"What if ours did?"

"The astronomers know a lot about novas," I said. "More than you'd guess. They can see them coming months ahead. Sol is a gee-naught yellow dwarf. They don't go nova at all. They have to wander off the main sequence first, and that takes millions of years."

She pounded a fist softly on my back. We were cheek to cheek; I couldn't see her face. "I don't want to believe it. I don't dare. Stan, nothing like this has ever happened before. How can you know?"

"Something did."

"What? I don't believe it. We'd remember."

"Do you remember the first moon landing? Aldrin and Armstrong?"

"Of course. We watched it at Earl's Lunar Landing Party."

"They landed on the biggest, flattest place they could find on the moon. They sent back several hours of jumpy home movies, took a lot of very clear pictures, left corrugated footprints all over the place. And they came home with a bunch of rocks.

"Remember? People said it was a long way to go for rocks. But the first thing anyone noticed about those rocks was that they were half melted.

"Sometime in the past, oh, say the past hundred thousand years; there's no way of marking it closer than that—the sun flared up. It didn't stay hot enough long enough to leave any marks on the Earth. But the moon doesn't have an atmosphere to protect it. All the rocks melted on one side."

The air was warm and damp. I took off my coat, which was heavy with rainwater. I fished the cigarettes and matches out, lit a cigarette and exhaled past Leslie's ear.

"We'd remember. It *couldn't* have been this bad."

"I'm not so sure. Suppose it happened over the Pacific? It wouldn't do *that* much damage. Or over the American continents. It would have sterilized some plants and animals and burned down a lot of forests, and who'd know? The sun went back to normal, that time. It might again. The sun is a four percent variable star. Maybe it gets a touch more variable than that, every so often."

Something shattered in the bedroom. A window? A wet wind touched us, and the shriek of the storm was louder.

"Then we could live through this," Leslie said hesitantly.

"I believe you've put your finger on the crux of the matter. Skol!" I found my champagne and drank deep. It was past three in the morning, with a hurricane beating at our doors.

"Then shouldn't we be doing something about it?"

"We are."

"Something like trying to get up into the hills! Stan, there're going to be floods!"

"You bet your ass there are, but they won't rise this high. Fourteen stories. Listen, I've thought this through. We're in a building that was designed to be earthquake proof. You told me so yourself. It'd take more than a hurricane to knock it over.

"As for heading for the hills, what hills? We won't get far tonight, not with the streets flooded already. Suppose we could get up into the Santa Monica Mountains; then what? Mudslides, that's what. That area won't stand up to what's coming. The flare must have boiled away enough water to make another ocean.

It's going to rain for forty days and forty nights! Love, this is the safest place we could have reached tonight."

"Suppose the polar caps melt?"

"Yeah . . . well, we're pretty high, even for that. Hey, maybe that last flare was what started Noah's Flood. Maybe it's happening again. Sure as hell, there's not a place on Earth that isn't the middle of a hurricane. Those two great counterrotating hurricanes, by now they must have broken up into hundreds of little storms—"

The glass doors exploded inward. We ducked, and the wind howled about us and dropped rain and glass on us.

"At least we've got food!" I shouted. "If the floods maroon us here, we can last it out!"

"But if the power goes, we can't cook it! And the refrigerator—"

"We'll cook everything we can. Hardboil all the eggs—"

The wind rose about us. I stopped trying to talk.

Warm rain sprayed us horizontally and left us soaked. Try to cook in a hurricane? I'd been stupid; I'd waited too long. The wind would tip boiling water on us if we tried it. Or hot grease—

Leslie screamed, "We'll have to use the oven!"

Of course. The oven couldn't possibly fall on us.

We set it for 400° and put the eggs in, in a pot of water. We took all the meat out of the meat drawer and shoved it in on a broiling pan. Two artichokes in another pot. The other vegetables we could eat raw.

What else? I tried to think.

Water. If the electricity went, probably the water and telephone lines would too. I turned on the faucet over the sink and started filling things: pots with lids, Leslie's thirty-cup percolator that she used for parties, her wash bucket. She clearly thought I was crazy, but I didn't trust the rain as a water source; I couldn't control it.

The sound. Already we'd stopped trying to shout through it. Forty days and nights of this and we'd be stone deaf. Cotton? Too late to reach the bathroom. Paper towels! I tore and wadded and made four plugs for our ears.

Sanitary facilities? Another reason for picking Leslie's place over mine. When the plumbing stopped, there was always the balcony.

And if the flood rose higher than the fourteenth floor, there was the roof. Twenty stories up. If it went higher than that, there would be damn few people left when it was over.

And if it was a nova?

I held Leslie a bit more closely, and lit another cigarette one-handed. All the wasted planning, if it was a nova. But I'd have been doing it anyway. You don't stop planning just because there's no hope.

And when the hurricane turned to live steam, there was always the balcony. At a dead run, and over the railing, in preference to being boiled alive.

But now was not the time to mention it.

Anyway, she'd probably thought of it herself.

The lights went out about four. I turned off the oven, in case the power should come back. Give it an hour to cool down, then I'd put all the food in Baggies.

Leslie was asleep, sitting up in my arms. How could she sleep, not knowing? I piled pillows behind her and let her back easy.

For some time I lay on my back, smoking, watching the lightning make shadows on the ceiling. We had eaten all the foie gras and drunk one bottle of champagne. I thought of opening the brandy, but decided against it, with regret.

A long time passed. I'm not sure what I thought about. I didn't sleep, but certainly my mind was in idle. It only gradually came to me that the ceiling, between lightning flashes, had turned grey.

I rolled over, gingerly, soggily. Everything was wet.

My watch said it was nine thirty.

I crawled around the partition into the living room. I'd been ignoring the storm sounds for so long that it took a faceful of warm whipping rain to remind me. There was a hurricane going on. But charcoal-grey light was filtering through the black clouds.

So. I was right to have saved the brandy. Floods, storms, intense radiation, fires lit by the flare—if the toll of destruction was as high as I expected, then money was about to become worthless. We would need trade goods.

I was hungry. I ate two eggs and some bacon—still warm—and started putting the rest of the food away. We had food for a week, maybe . . . but hardly a balanced diet. Maybe we could trade with other apartments. This was a big building. There must be empty apartments, too, that we could raid for canned soup and the like. And refugees from the lower floors to be taken care of, if the waters rose high enough . . .

Damn! I missed the nova. Life had been simplicity itself last night. Now . . . Did we have medicines? Were there doctors in the building? There would be dysentery and other plagues. And hunger. There was a supermarket near here; could we find a scuba rig in the building?

But I'd get some sleep first. Later we could start exploring the building. The day had become a lighter charcoal grey. Things could be worse, far worse. I thought of the radiation that must have sleeted over the far side of the world, and wondered if our children would colonize Europe, or Asia, or Africa.

WHAT CAN YOU SAY ABOUT
CHOCOLATE COVERED
MANHOLE COVERS?

It was the last party. Otherwise it was only one of many, so many that they merged in the memory. We all knew each other. George had invited around thirty of us, a heterogeneous group, aged from teen to retirement, in dress that varied from hippie to mod to jeans and sneakers to dark suits, and hair that varied from crew cut to shoulder length.

It was a divorce party.

Granted that it's been done before, still it was done well. George and Dina had planned it a year earlier, to celebrate the night their Decree became Final. The cake was frosted in black, and was surmounted by the usual wax figures, but facing outward from opposite edges of the cake. Jack Keenan donned a minister's reversed collar to officiate. His makeshift sacrament included part of the funniest prayer in literature: the agnostic's prayer from Zelazny's *Creatures of Light and Darkness*. George and Dina kissed with obvious sincerity, for the last time, and everybody clapped like mad.

Afterward I got coffee and a piece of divorce cake and found a flat place to set them. Without a third hand to handle the plastic fork, I was as good as trapped there; and there it was that Tom Findlay found me.

Tom Findlay was all red hair and beard. The beard was full and thick, the hair long enough to tie in back with a rubber band. Once he had gone to a costume party with his hair combed forward over his eyes and the bridge of his nose, and a placard around his neck that read NOT A SHEEP DOG. He generally wore knee-length socks and leather shorts. His legs too were thickly covered with red hair. He spoke in a slow midwestern drawl, and grinned constantly, as if he were watching very funny pictures inside his head.

He was always part of these groups. Once a month he held a BYOB party of his own. He had a tendency to monopolize a conversation; but even those who avoided him on that account had to admit that he gave fair warning. He would walk up to any friend or stranger he found standing alone and open conversation with, "Hey. Would a Muslim vampire be terrified of a copy of the Koran?"

Or, "It seems to me that anarchy would be a very unstable form of government, don't you think?"

Or, "What about chocolate covered manhole covers?"

That one fell pretty flat, I remember. What can anyone say about chocolate covered manhole covers? Most of Findlay's ideas were at least worth discussing. Vampires, for instance. What significance has the vampire's religion? Or the victim's blood type? Could you hold off a vampire with a sunlamp, or kill him with a stake of grained plastic wood? If a bullet won't kill a vampire, what about a revolver loaded with a blank cartridge and a wooden pencil?

And one night someone had come running in to interrupt the poker game in the other room. "What do you think Findlay just came up with?" And it was a new form of ice skating. You strap blocks of ice to your feet, see, and you skate over a field of razor blades set on edge.

Wild? Consider the ramifications! Straps will be cut, unless you embed them in the ice itself. God help you if you take a spill, or let the ice melt too far. And the blades have to be lined up. So how can you change directions? The only answer to that one is to lay the blades in a loop, like a skating rink.

That night, the night of the divorce party, Findlay perched on the edge of the table I was using for my cup and plate, and said, "Hey. Suppose all the Adam and Eve legends were true?"

I could have gotten away, but it would have meant finding another flat spot. I said, "That story's been done to death. A rocket ship crashes on Earth, see, with two people aboard—"

"No, no, you don't take my meaning. Every big and little group in the world, past and present, has a creation myth." Findlay's midwest accent did odd things to the two dollar words he was fond of using. "They all involve one man and one woman. In every case all of humanity sprang from that one couple. Suppose they were *all* true?"

My wife moved up from behind me and slid one arm around my waist. "You mean five hundred different Edens? That wouldn't make sense." She nestled against me, unobtrusively, feeling warm and silky in a loose, flowing pant dress.

Findlay turned to her eagerly. "Carol, do you know anything about breeding horses? Or cattle?"

"Dogs. My mother raises keeshonden."

We didn't see where he was going, but Findlay seemed to sense we were hooked. He settled himself more comfortably on the table. "There's a stock method of improving a breed. It always works, but it takes a long time. How long depends on what you're trying to improve, of course.

"Suppose you're working with horses, just for argument. You've got a hundred horses for base stock. What you do is, you fence them off into say twenty-five corrals of four horses each. A large number of small groups. You make them breed within the group.

"Pretty quick you get severe inbreeding. All the little deadly recessive traits start to come out, and combine. You lose a lot of each generation. You help it along by weeding out the traits you don't like, like blindness or early senility.

"You keep it up for as many generations as you've got time for. Then you run them all together. You know how hybrid vigor works?"

"It's a mathematical thing, really," someone muttered deprecatingly. I realized that we'd acquired an audience. Four or five male teens were standing around listening, attracted either by Findlay's carrying voice or by my wife, who is uncommonly pretty. They were looking puzzled but interested, except for the one who had spoken.

Hal Grant was a small, dark fifteen-year-old with an astonishing vocabulary. With his full black beard and collar-length hair he looked like a young baron out of the Middle Ages; but he talked like a college professor. People tended to see him as an adult, and to react with astonishment on the rare occasions when he acted like a fifteen-year-old.

When nobody tried to stop him, he went on. "Say you've got a strain of horses that has a dominant for weak eyes, and another that has weak hindquarters. You breed a stallion from one strain to a mare from the other strain until you get four colts. In general one colt won't have either of the bad traits, one will have the weak eyes, one will have weak hindquarters, and one will have both. That's straight Mendelian genetics. Where the hybrid vigor comes in is, the one with both of the bad traits can't compete. He dies. That leaves three colts, and one is an improvement over both his parents. The average quality goes up."

Findlay was nodding his approval. "Right. That's how it works. So you run all the horses together. A lot of the weak traits that didn't get killed off in the interbreeding phase, combine and kill their owners. You wind up with a superior strain of horses."

"It wouldn't work with dogs," said Carol. "Mongrels don't win dog shows."

"But in a fair fight they tend to kill the winners," Hal pointed out.

"The technique works on just about anything," said Findlay. "Horses, dogs, cattle, chinchillas. Split the base stock into small groups, make them interbreed for several generations, then run them all together. Now keep it in mind, and we'll make some assumptions.

"We assume an alien race, and we assume they've got a pet that's almost bright enough to make a good servant. Its hands can hold a serving tray. They could almost repair machinery—"

"Homo habilis," said somebody.

"Right. You have to assume the overlord race had a lot of time, and endless patience—"

"And cheap space travel."

"Wouldn't have to be faster than light, though. Not if they had all that endless patience." We could see where Findlay was going now, and everyone wanted to get there first. Hence the interruptions.

Findlay said, "So they pick out about a thousand of the brightest of their animals, and they split them up into pairs, male and female. They find an Earthlike world and set down five hundred couples in five hundred locations."

"Then the Noah legend—"

"Came first," I said. "And you get five hundred Edens. Beautiful."

"Right. Now look at how it works. Each of the little groups undergoes severe inbreeding. They're all cut off from each other by fences of one kind or another, mountains, rivers, deserts. The recessive traits come out, and some of the groups die off completely. Others spread out.

"Remember, it's the most successful ones that are spreading. They infringe on other groups. The genes start to mix. The quality of the mix goes up, partly because of hybrid vigor. If they're going to develop intelligence, this is where it starts."

"Hah! They'd start inventing ways around the

fences," said an older kid. Short blond hair, pale fringe of mustache, knitted sailing cap surgically attached to his head; I forget his name. "Bridges across the rivers, canteens for the deserts—"

"And camels."

"Passes across the mountains. Ways to tell each other how to find them."

"Ships!"

"Right," said Findlay, his blue eyes glowing with pleasure. "Now notice that the most intelligent groups are the ones that spread their genes around the most, because they're the ones that do all the traveling. Also, the more inventions you get, the easier it is to mix; the more mixing you get, the higher the intelligence goes; and that makes for more inventions, like paved roads and better rigging for the ships and better breeds of horses. Eventually you get airplanes, busses, guided tours and printed language guides and international credit organizations."

"And tourist traps."

"And multilingual whores."

"Not to put a damper on any of this fun stuff," said Hal Grant, the dark youth with the very adult vocabulary, "but eventually they'll be coming back to see how we're doing."

"How would they know when we're ready?" someone wondered. "Just stop by for a look every thousand years?"

Hal said, "Not good enough. Look how far we've come in the last five hundred years. Give us another five hundred and we'll be competitors, not slaves."

"Or dead of pollution."

"But they wouldn't have to check. They just wait until—"

"Project Ozma!"

"But how could they be sure we'd signal *them*?"

"They must be in one of the nearby stellar systems. Alpha Centauri, Tau Ceti—"

"Or they left signal devices in all the likely systems—"

"Wouldn't it depend on how intelligent they want us? Maybe we're supposed to be repairmen for a starship motor. Then they—"

"They'd damn well wait for *us* to come to *them*, wouldn't they? To prove we can build a starship!"

Jack Keenan tapped me on the shoulder. He was still wearing his clerical collar. He spoke low, near my ear. "There's a place at the poker table. They sent me to tell you."

My cake was gone, and the conversation here was turning chaotic. I got up. Behind me Tom Findlay was saying, "But they'd have to *find* our starships some way. Maybe a large metallic mass moving faster than light would put out heavy Cherenkov radiation . . ."

I played for an hour and lost a dollar twenty. Presently Carol put her head around the corner, caught my eye, showed her teeth and snapped them at me several times in rapid succession. I nodded and cashed in.

It means, "I'm starving. Let's collect some people and go eat."

There was still a group around Tom Findlay. I caught bits and pieces of sentences. They were talking about the things you could do with neutronium, if you could get it in four foot globs and had the technology to move it around. I broke in to ask if anyone was hungry, and got Hal Grant that way.

We looked up our host (our hostess had gone home with her date), thanked him for a great party, told him we might be back in an hour or so, and asked if he'd like to come along. The guests could take care of themselves, and he knew it, but he declined anyway.

Joy Benjamin was outside sitting on the wall, breathing. There was precious little oxygen left inside. She joined us too. We drove off to find a place we knew of, an all-night pizza place.

Sometimes they get forgotten instantly. Sometimes they go on and on. This latest of Findlay's brainstorms was one of Those. I came back from the counter carrying a tremendous deluxe pizza, and Hal Grant was saying, "See, that way you wouldn't need a Project Ozma, or an FTL spacecraft detector either." And both women were nodding, rapt.

Joy Benjamin was young and pretty and a bit pudgy, and her front teeth showed when she smiled. It all gave her a cuddly, innocent look that I had never found occasion to mention to my wife; but if she had been in the group around Findlay I would have noticed her. She must have gotten her details at second hand. She looked up as I set the pizza down, and said, "He's got a point. You know about Tom Findlay's Multiple Eden Hypothesis?"

"Yes."

"This planet puts out as much radio flux as a small star," she said seriously. "The overlords could put a detector on the Moon and then just wait for us to invent radios."

"That means they must be on their way here now," my wife put in.

Hal smiled sardonically, an effect he couldn't have managed without the beard. "Maybe they're already here. There were flying saucers all over the place when radio was *really* popular, before everybody had two television sets."

"It's been done, that bit about a detector on the Moon. In *2001*. Put it on Mars."

"Okay, it's on Mars. The point is, with the radio detector they can get here after we develop as much intelligence as we're going to, but before we can pollute ourselves to death or bomb ourselves to death. After all, they probably weren't trying to develop anything *supremely* intelligent. Just bright enough to take orders."

"How young you are, to be so cynical."

It took him a moment to decide I was kidding. He

said, "Someday, Howards," and shook his head sorrowfully, contemplating awful carnage. He went to work on the pizza.

It was delicious. I wish I'd paid more attention, because it was the last time I ever tasted pizza. We ate on a wooden bench, and used up an inch-high stack of paper napkins. Off in one corner, a man with garters on his sleeves played a player piano.

"So we can expect them any minute." Joy made whirring noises and moved her hands expressively. "Big ships in the sky, coming down to ssscoop us up."

"Or little ships to take samples."

"If they were the flying saucers, they must have rejected us already," Hal put in. "They've been here too long. They'd have started major scooping operations long ago."

And if we'd dropped it there, we'd be home now.

There are tunes that go round and round in your head, driving you nuts, driving others nuts because you're humming under your breath. There are ideas you can't leave alone. You toy with them, or they toy with you . . . I got my fair share of the pizza and a bit more. While we were waiting for Carol to finish, I said, "Suppose they did reject us. Suppose we didn't meet their presumably exacting standards. What then?"

"They'd destroy the Earth," Joy said instantly.

"Typical bloodthirsty female."

Hal said, "Maybe they'd start us over. Give us IQ tests. Pick a thousand off the top. Settle us on a new planet."

"*Then* destroy the Earth."

"Maybe. Maybe even settle us back on Earth, after clearing it for us."

Grant's "us" had not escaped me. He would be one of the thousand, and so would his friends. I let it pass. Truth to tell, I was flattered.

The pizza was gone, and much of the cardboard disc beneath it. We piled in the car and started back to George's place.

Carol ended a reflective silence. "Does it seem to anyone that there are more written tests around than there used to be? Army IQ tests, motivational research, testing for jobs, even the forms for computer dating. Now—"

We started laughing. Hal said, "Are you still on that?"

"Well, they have to test us *some* way."

"It's a lovely idea, but I can't bring myself to trust those IQ tests. I know too much psychology. There's not a printed test that's good for anything, especially at the top of the scale."

"What, then?"

"There Are Aliens Among Us," Hal Grant intoned. "Or their agents. And they choose by intuition and superior judgment. You, and you—"

"Hey," I said, hit by a lovely idea. "Hey. You know who would make a great intelligence tester?"

"Who?"

"Tom Findlay! He's a walking, talking intelligence test. Remember what he was talking about just before we left? Blobs of neutron star matter—"

"That's lovely stuff, neutronium. It's unreasonably heavy. If you just let it sit, it's *got* to be a shiny sphere. The surface gravity would flatten any surface roughness, see? If you toss a glob of the stuff at an enemy spaceship, it'll just *drift* through the hull and leave a gaping hole and come out a fraction of an inch thicker. Spin it and you don't get an ellipsoid, you get like a flying saucer, a ball with a rim around it. It's all theoretical, of course."

"See what I mean?"

Behind me in the darkened car, Hal Grant said, "I guess so. Findlay makes you think. If you can't think, you go away. After awhile there's nobody left talking to Findlay except people who like playing with ideas. He's a filter. Then I suppose he tags the best of us and off we go, right?"

"Right. Well, nobody's disappeared yet."

"Nobody that was noticed. How many of us do you know, away from these parties? Sometimes I run across Jack Keenan in the supermarket, but that's it. All we know for sure is, *we* haven't been picked yet." Grant laughed uneasily. "Maybe we'd better not go back to George's."

The feel of the car changed drastically. I hit the brake fast, but it was hardly necessary; we were only starting to move from a dead stop. A moment ago we'd been doing seventy.

I heard the sea before I saw it: breakers crunching ahead of us, flashing white in the headlights. If I'd kept the throttle down we'd have driven right into them. The freeway lighting had become a pale pink glow far across the sea; dawn or dusk, I couldn't tell. We were in soft dry sand. It might have been a California beach, and our car sitting mired in sand might have been a television commercial or a practical joke, except that it wasn't.

"S-s-sonofabitch took me at my word," said Hal Grant. Then, "This can't be real. Can it?"

Joy was furious. "He was *listening* to us! That— eavesdropper!"

I got out.

It felt like sand. It crunched beneath my feet, like sand. How could it be part of another world? But the sinking feeling in my belly felt like an elevator starting down. Terror? Or low gravity?

I threw back my head and screamed, "Findlay!"

And he was there, grinning out of a metal cagework affair. "Figured it out, did you?"

"Christ no, Findlay! What's going on here? We're terribly confused! One minute we were driving along the freeway, and the next we're here at Hermosa Beach!"

First he was flabbergasted. Then he burst out laughing. Well, it had been worth a try.

So was my next move. His head was thrown back and his beard was raised, and I stepped forward fast and hit him in the throat, putting all my weight behind it.

Not murder. Justice. And we needed that cage affair to get home.

It was like hitting a padded pillar. My head snapped forward, my teeth came together with a sharp click, and something gave agonizingly in my shoulder. Tom Findlay must have weighed over a ton.

He stopped laughing, gradually. "Very good. Nobody's ever adjusted quite that fast. Let's say you pass with honors," he said. "And here's your diploma."

It appeared beside him in the cage: a black disc on edge, two feet high. He caught it before it could topple, and he sent it rolling out. I let it go past me.

Grant had come up behind me. In resignation he said, "Where are we?"

"A lot of use you'll get out of that! I'll tell you anyway. It's the second planet out from Alpha Centauri A. If you were hoping for double suns and wild new constellations, you can forget it. We used the closest available water world."

"Gonna be dull," said Hal. He'd given up.

So had I. I inhaled; the air smelled incredibly clean. A door slammed behind me. The women. God, don't let them beg. I said, "So they came and sampled us and found us wanting. So they're doing it over with another five hundred Edens. So where do you come in, Findlay? They aren't human, are they?"

"Not by a long way," said Findlay, with reverence. "Neither am I. I'm a robot. I'm also the ideal they're aiming for, in case you were wondering."

"I wasn't."

"Now, now."

"If you're just what they want, why do they need us?"

"I'm expensive. Robots don't breed. You can forget about genetic engineering, too. It's immoral. I don't know why. It's enough that they think so. Anything else?"

"We were doing seventy on the freeway," said Hal. "What happened to the momentum?"

"You were also doing about twenty miles per second with respect to this beach. We just took it all in one vector sum. What else? Oh, you won't be separated. This Eden will hold all four of you. We did it that way last time, too. The Eden story is only a myth."

"Are there any others?" Carol cried. "What direction are they."

But he was gone, and the metal frame around him. We were alone on a beach, four of us and a car, in the growing light of dawn.

"This thing is *sticky*," Hal said suddenly. He was holding the black disc that Findlay had rolled past me. He looked at his hand, then licked a finger. "Right. It's a memento, his signature, as it were. What can you say about chocolate covered manhole covers?"

"Don't get it sandy," my wife said briskly. "We can eat the chocolate. It's the only thing on this world that we know we can eat."

BECALMED IN HELL

I could feel the heat hovering outside. In the cabin it was bright and dry and cool, almost too cool, like a modern office building in the dead of summer. Beyond the two small windows it was as black as it ever gets in the solar system, and hot enough to melt lead, at a pressure equivalent to three hundred feet beneath the ocean.

"There goes ·a fish," I said, just to break the monotony.

"So how's it cooked?"

"Can't tell. It seems to be leaving a trail of bread-crumbs. Fried? Imagine that, Eric! A fried jellyfish."

Eric sighed noisily. "Do I have to?"

"You have to. Only way you'll see anything worth-while in this—this—" Soup? Fog? Boiling maple syrup?

"Searing black calm."

"Right."

"Someone dreamed up that phrase when I was a kid, just after the news of the Mariner II probe. An eternal searing black calm, hot as a kiln, under an atmosphere thick enough to keep any light or any breath of wind from ever reaching the surface."

I shivered. "What's the outside temperature now?"

"You'd rather not know. You've always had too much imagination, Howie."

"I can take it, Doc."

"Six hundred and twelve degrees."

"I can't take it, Doc!"

This was Venus, planet of Love, favorite of the

science-fiction writers of three decades ago. Our ship
hung below the Earth-to-Venus hydrogen fuel tank,
twenty miles up and all but motionless in the syrupy
air. The tank, nearly empty now, made an excellent
blimp. It would keep us aloft as long as the internal
pressure matched the external. That was Eric's job,
to regulate the tank's pressure by regulating the temperature of the hydrogen gas. We had collected air
samples after each ten mile drop from three hundred
miles on down, and temperature readings for shorter
intervals, and we had dropped the small probe. The
data we had gotten from the surface merely con-
firmed in detail our previous knowledge of the hottest
world in the solar system.

"Temperature just went up to six-thirteen," said
Eric. "Look, are you through bitching?"

"For the moment."

"Good. Strap down. We're taking off."

"Oh, frabjous day!" I started untangling the crash
webbing over my couch.

"We've done everything we came to do. Haven't we?"

"Am I arguing? Look, I'm strapped down."

"Yeah."

I knew why he was reluctant to leave. I felt a touch
of it myself. We'd spent four months getting to Venus
in order to spend a week circling her and less than two
days in her upper atmosphere, and it seemed a terrible
waste of time.

But he was taking too long. "What's the trouble,
Eric?"

"You'd rather not know."

He meant it. His voice was a mechanical, inhuman
monotone; he wasn't making the extra effort to get
human expression out of his "prosthetic" vocal appa-
ratus. Only a severe shock would affect him that way.

"I can take it," I said.

"Okay. I can't feel anything in the ramjet controls.
Feels like I've just had a spinal anesthetic."

The cold in the cabin drained into me, all of it. "See

if you can send motor impulses the other way. You could run the rams by guess-and-hope even if you can't feel them."

"Okay." One split second later, "They don't. Nothing happens. Good thinking though."

I tried to think of something to say while I untied myself from the couch. What came out was, "It's been a pleasure knowing you, Eric. I've liked being half of this team, and I still do."

"Get maudlin later. Right now, start checking my attachments. Carefully."

I swallowed my comments and went to open the access door in the cabin's forward wall. The floor swayed ever so gently beneath my feet.

Beyond the four-foot-square access door was Eric. Eric's central nervous system, with the brain perched at the top and the spinal cord coiled in a loose spiral to fit more compactly into the transparent glass-and-sponge-plastic housing. Hundreds of wires from all over the ship led to the glass walls, where they were joined to selected nerves which spread like an electrical network from the central coil of nervous tissue and fatty protective membrane.

Space leaves no cripples; and don't call Eric a cripple, because he doesn't like it. In a way he's the ideal spaceman. His life support system weighs only half what mine does, and takes up a twelfth as much room. But his other prosthetic aids take up most of the ship. The ramjets were hooked into the last pair of nerve trunks, the nerves which once moved his legs, and dozens of finer nerves in those trunks sensed and regulated fuel feed, ram temperature, differential acceleration, intake aperture dilation, and spark pulse.

These connections were intact. I checked them four different ways without finding the slightest reason why they shouldn't be working.

"Test the others," said Eric.

It took a good two hours to check every trunk nerve connection. They were all solid. The blood pump was chugging along, and the fluid was rich enough, which killed the idea that the ram nerves might have "gone to sleep" from lack of nutrients or oxygen. Since the lab is one of his prosthetic aids, I let Eric analyse his own blood sugar, hoping that the "liver" had goofed and was producing some other sugar compound. The conclusions were appalling. There was nothing wrong with Eric—inside the cabin.

"Eric, you're healthier than I am."

"I could tell. You look worried, and I don't blame you. Now you'll have to go outside."

"I know. Let's dig out the suit."

It was in the emergency tools locker, the Venus suit that was never supposed to be used. NASA had designed it for use at Venusian ground level. Then they had refused to okay the ship below twenty miles until they knew more about the planet. The suit was a segmented armor job. I had watched it being tested in the heat-and-pressure box at Cal Tech, and I knew that the joints stopped moving after five hours, and wouldn't start again until they had been cooled. Now I opened the locker and pulled the suit out by the shoulders and held it in front of me. It seemed to be staring back.

"You still can't feel anything in the ramjets?"

"Not a twinge."

I started to put on the suit, piece by piece like medieval armor. Then I thought of something else. "We're twenty miles up. Are you going to ask me to do a balancing act on the hull?"

"No! Wouldn't think of it. We'll just have to go down."

The lift from the blimp tank was supposed to be constant until takeoff. When the time came Eric could get extra lift by heating the hydogen to higher pressure, then cracking a valve to let the excess out. Of course he'd have to be very careful that the pressure was higher in the tank, or we'd get venusian air coming in, and the ship would fall instead of rising. Naturally that would be disastrous.

So Eric lowered the tank temperature and cracked the valve, and down we went.

"Of course there's a catch," said Eric.

"I know."

"The ship stood the pressure twenty miles up. At ground level it'll be six times that."

"I know."

We fell fast, with the cabin tilted forward by the drag on our tailfins. The temperature rose gradually. The pressure went up fast. I sat at the window and saw nothing, nothing but black, but I sat there anyway and waited for the window to crack. NASA had refused to okay the ship below twenty miles . . .

Eric said, "The blimp tank's okay, and so's the ship, I think. But will the cabin stand up to it?"

"I wouldn't know."

"Ten miles."

Five hundred miles above us, unreachable, was the atomic ion engine that was to take us home. We couldn't get to it on the chemical rocket alone. The rocket was for use after the air become too thin for the ramjets.

"Four miles. Have to crack the valve again."

The ship dropped.

"I can see ground," said Eric.

I couldn't. Eric caught me straining my eyes and said, "Forget it. I'm using deep infrared, and getting no detail."

"No vast, misty swamps with weird, terrifying monsters and man eating plants?"

"All I see is hot, bare dirt."

But we were almost down, and there were no cracks in the cabin wall. My neck and shoulder muscles loosened. I turned away from the window. Hours had passed while we dropped through the poisoned, thickening air. I already had most of my suit on. Now I screwed on my helmet and three-finger gauntlets.

"Strap down," said Eric. I did.

We bumped gently. The ship tilted a little, swayed back, bumped again. And again, with my teeth rattling and my armor-plated body rolling against the crash webbing. "Damn," Eric muttered. I heard the hiss from above. Eric said, "I don't know how we'll get back up."

Neither did I. The ship bumped hard and stayed down, and I got up and went to the airlock.

"Good luck," said Eric. "Don't stay out too long." I waved at his cabin camera. The outside temperature was seven hundred and thirty.

The outer door opened. My suit refrigerating unit set up a complaining whine. With an empty bucket in each hand, and with my headlamp blazing a way through the black murk, I stepped out onto the right wing.

My suit creaked and settled under the pressure, and I stood on the wing and waited for it to stop. It was almost like being under water. My headlamp beam went out thick enough to be solid, penetrating no more than a hundred feet. The air couldn't have been that opaque, no matter how dense. It must have been full of dust, or tiny droplets of some fluid.

The wing ran back like a knife-edged running board, widening toward the tail to where it spread into a tailfin. The two tailfins met back of the fuselage. At each tailfin tip was the ram, a big sculptured cylinder with an atomic engine inside. It wouldn't be hot because it hadn't been used yet, but I had my counter anyway.

I fastened a line to the wing and slid to the ground. As long as we were *here* . . . The ground turned out to be a dry, reddish dirt, crumbly, and so porous that it was almost spongy. Lava etched by chemicals? Almost anything would be corrosive at this pressure and temperature. I scooped one pailful from the surface and another from underneath the first, then climbed up the line and left the buckets on the wing.

The wing was terribly slippery. I had to wear mag-

netic sandals to stay on. I walked up and back along
the two-hundred-foot length of the ship, making a
casual inspection. Neither wing nor fuselage showed
damage. Why not? If a meteor or something had cut
Eric's contact with his sensors in the rams, there should
have been evidence of a break in the surface.

Then, almost suddenly, I realized that there was an
alternative.

It was too vague a suspicion to put into words yet,
and I still had to finish the inspection. Telling Eric
would be very difficult if I was right.

Four inspection panels were set into the wing, well
protected from the reentry heat. One was halfway back
on the fuselage, below the lower edge of the blimp
tank, which was molded to the fuselage in such a way
that from the front the ship looked like a dolphin. Two
more were in the trailing edge of the tailfin and the
fourth was in the ram itself. All opened, with powered
screwdriver on recessed screws, on junctions of the
ship's electrical system.

There was nothing out of place under any of the
panels. By making and breaking contacts and getting
Eric's reactions, I found that his sensation ended somewhere between the second and third inspection panels.
It was the same story on the left wing. No external
damage, nothing wrong at the junctions. I climbed back
to ground and walked slowly beneath the length of
each wing, my headlamp tilted up. No damage underneath.

I collected my buckets and went back inside.

"A bone to pick?" Eric was puzzled. "Isn't this a
strange time to start an argument? Save it for space.
We'll have four months with nothing else to do."

"This can't wait. First of all, did you notice anything
I didn't?" He'd been watching everything I saw and
did through the peeper in my helmet.

"No. I'd have yelled."

"Okay. Now get this.

"The break in your circuits isn't inside, because you get sensation up to the second wing inspection panels. It isn't outside because there's no evidence of damage, not even corrosion spots. That leaves only one place for the flaw."

"Go on."

"We also have the puzzle of why you're paralyzed in both rams. Why should they both go wrong at the same time? There's only one place in the ship where the circuits join."

"What? Oh, yes, I see. They joined through me."

"Now let's assume for the moment that you're the piece of equipment with the flaw in it. You're not a piece of machinery, Eric. If something's wrong with you it isn't medical. That was the first thing we covered. But it could be psychological."

"It's nice to know you think I'm human. So I've slipped a cam, have I?"

"Slightly. I think you've got a case of what used to be called trigger anesthesia. A soldier who kills too often sometimes finds that his right index finger or even his whole hand has gone numb, as if it were no longer a part of him. Your comment about not being a machine is important, Eric. I think that's the whole problem. You've never really believed that any part of the ship is a part of *you*. That's intelligent, because it's true. Every time the ship is redesigned you get a new set of parts, and it's right to avoid thinking of a change of model as a series of amputations." I'd been rehearsing this speech, trying to put it so that Eric would have no choice but to believe me. Now I know that it must have sounded phoney. "But now you've gone too far. Subconsciously you've stopped believing that the rams can *feel* like a part of you, which they were designed to do. So you've persuaded yourself that you don't feel anything."

With my prepared speech done, and nothing left to say, I stopped talking and waited for the explosion.

"You make good sense," said Eric.

I was staggered. "You agree?"

"I didn't say that. You spin an elegant theory, but I want time to think about it. What do we do if it's true?"

"Why . . . I don't know. You'll just have to cure yourself."

"Okay. Now here's *my* idea. I propose that you thought up this theory to relieve yourself of a responsibility for getting us home alive. It puts the whole problem in my lap, metaphorically speaking."

"Oh, for—"

"Shut up. I haven't said you're wrong. That would be an ad hominem argument. We need time to think about this."

It was lights-out, four hours later, before Eric would return to the subject.

"Howie, do me a favor. Assume for awhile that something mechanical is causing all our trouble. I'll assume it's psychosomatic."

"Seems reasonable."

"It is reasonable. What can you do if I've gone psychosomatic? What can I do if it's mechanical? I can't go around inspecting myself. We'd each better stick to what we know."

"It's a deal." I turned him off for the night and went to bed.

But not to sleep.

With the lights off it was just like outside. I turned them back on. It wouldn't wake Eric. Eric never sleeps normally, since his blood doesn't accumulate fatigue poisons, and he'd go mad from being awake all the time if he didn't have a Russian sleep inducer plate near his cortex. The ship could implode without waking Eric when his sleep inducer's on. But I felt foolish being afraid of the dark.

While the dark stayed outside it was all right.

But it wouldn't stay there. It had invaded my partner's mind. Because his chemical checks guard him against chemical insanities like schizophrenia, we'd assumed he was permanently sane. But how could any prosthetic device protect him from his own imagination, his own misplaced common sense?

I couldn't keep my bargain. I knew I was right. But what could I do about it?

Hindsight is wonderful. I could see exactly what our mistake had been, Eric's and mine and the hundreds of men who had built his life support after the crash. There was nothing left of Eric then except the intact central nervous system, and no glands except the pituitary. "We'll regulate his blood composition," they said, "and he'll always be cool, calm and collected. No panic reactions from Eric!"

I know a girl whose father had an accident when he was forty-five or so. He was out with his brother, the girl's uncle, on a fishing trip. They were blind drunk when they started home, and the guy was riding on the hood while the brother drove. Then the brother made a sudden stop. Our hero left two important glands on the hood ornament.

The only change in his sex life was that his wife stopped worrying about late pregnancy. His *habits* were developed.

Eric doesn't need adrenal glands to be afraid of death. His emotional patterns were fixed long before the day he tried to land a moonship without radar. He'd grab any excuse to believe that I'd fixed whatever was wrong with the ram connections.

But he was counting on me to do it.

The atmosphere leaned on the windows. Not wanting to, I reached out to touch the quartz with my fingertips. I couldn't feel the pressure. But it was there, inexorable as the tide smashing a rock into sand grains. How long would the cabin hold it back?

If some broken part were holding us here, how could I have missed finding it? Perhaps it had left no break in the surface of either wing. But how?

That was an angle.

Two cigarettes later I got up to get the sample

buckets. They were empty, the alien dirt safely stored away. I filled them with water and put them in the cooler, set the cooler for 40° Absolute, then turned off the lights and went to bed.

The morning was blacker than the inside of a smoker's lungs. What Venus really needs, I decided, philosophizing on my back, is to lose ninety-nine percent of her air. That would give her a bit more than half as much air as Earth, which would lower the greenhouse effect enough to make the temperature livable. Drop Venus' gravity to near zero for a few weeks and the work would do itself.

The whole damn universe is waiting for us to discover antigravity.

"Morning," said Eric. "Thought of anything?"

"Yes." I rolled out of bed. "Now don't bug me with questions. I'll explain everything as I go."

"No breakfast?"

"Not yet."

Piece by piece I put my suit on, just like one of King Arthur's gentlemen, and went for the buckets only after the gauntlets were on. The ice, in the cold section, was in the chilly neighborhood of absolute zero. "This is two buckets of ordinary ice," I said, holding them up. "Now let me out."

"I should keep you here till you talk," Eric groused. But the doors opened and I went out onto the wing. I started talking while I unscrewed the number two right panel.

"Eric, think a moment about the tests they run on a manned ship before they'll let a man walk into the lifesystem. They test every part separately and in conjunction with other parts. Yet if something isn't working, either it's damaged or it wasn't tested right. Right?"

"Reasonable." He wasn't giving away anything.

"Well, nothing caused any damage. Not only is there no break in the ship's skin, but no coincidence could have made both rams go haywire at the same time. So something wasn't tested right."

I had the panel off. In the buckets the ice boiled gently where it touched the surfaces of the glass buckets. The blue ice cakes had cracked under their own internal pressure. I dumped one bucket into the maze of wiring and contacts and relays, and the ice shattered, giving me room to close the panel.

"So I thought of something last night, something that wasn't tested. Every part of the ship must have been in the heat-and-pressure box, exposed to artificial Venus conditions, but the ship as a whole, a unit, couldn't have been. It's too big." I'd circled around to the left wing and was opening the number three panel in the trailing edge. My remaining ice was half water and half small chips; I sloshed these in and fastened the panel. "What cut your circuits must have been the heat or the pressure or both. I can't help the pressure, but I'm cooling these relays with ice. Let me know which ram gets its sensation back first, and we'll know which inspection panel is the right one."

"Howie. Has it occurred to you what the cold water might do to those hot metals?"

"It could crack them. Then you'd lose all control over the ramjets, which is what's wrong right now."

"Uh. Your point, partner. But I still can't feel anything."

I went back to the airlock with my empty buckets swinging, wondering if they'd get hot enough to melt. They might have, but I wasn't out that long. I had my suit off and was refilling the buckets when Eric said, "I can feel the right ram."

"How extensive? Full control?"

"No, I can't feel the temperature. Oh, here it comes. We're all set, Howie."

My sigh of relief was sincere.

I put the buckets in the freezer again. We'd certainly want to take off with the relays cold. The water had been chilling for perhaps twenty minutes when Eric reported, "Sensation's going."

"What?"

"Sensation's going. No temperature, and I'm losing fuel feed control. It doesn't stay cold long enough."

"Ouch! Now what?"

"I hate to tell you. I'd almost rather let you figure it out for yourself."

I had. "We go as high as we can on the blimp tank, then I go out on the wing with a bucket of ice in each hand—"

We had to raise the blimp tank temperature to almost eight hundred degrees to get pressure, but from then on we went up in good shape. To sixteen miles. It took three hours.

"That's as high as we go," said Eric. "You ready?"

I went to get the ice. Eric could see me, he didn't need an answer. He opened the airlock for me.

Fear I might have felt, or panic, or determination or self sacrifice—but there was nothing. I went out feeling like a used zombie.

My magnets were on full. It felt like I was walking through shallow tar. The air was thick, though not as heavy as it had been down there. I followed my headlamp to the number two panel, opened it, poured ice in and threw the bucket high and far. The ice was in one cake. I couldn't close the panel. I left it open and hurried around to the other wing. The second bucket was filled with exploded chips; I sloshed them in and locked the number two left panel and came back with both hands free. It still looked like limbo in all directions, except where the headlamp cut a tunnel through the darkness, and—my feet were getting hot. I closed the right panel on boiling water and sidled back along the hull into the airlock.

"Come in and strap down," said Eric. "Hurry!"

"Gotta get my suit off." My hands had started to shake from reaction. I couldn't work the clamps.

"No you don't. If you start right now we may get home. Leave the suit on and come in."

I did. As I pulled my webbing shut, the rams roared. The ship shuddered a little, then pushed forward as we dropped from under the blimp tank. Pressure mounted as the rams reached operating speed. Eric was giving it all he had. It would have been uncomfortable even without the metal suit around me. With the suit on it was torture. My couch was afire from the suit, but I couldn't get breath to say so. We were going almost straight up.

We had gone twenty minutes when the ship jerked like a galvanized frog. "Ram's out," Eric said calmly. "I'll use the other." Another lurch as we dropped the dead one. The ship flew on like a wounded penguin, but still accelerating.

One minute . . . two . . .

The other ram quit. It was as if we'd run into molasses. Eric blew off the ram and the pressure eased. I could talk.

"Eric."

"What?"

"Got any marshmallows?"

"What? Oh, I see. Is your suit tight?"

"Sure."

"Live with it. We'll flush the smoke out later. I'm going to coast above some of this stuff, but when I use the rocket it'll be savage. No mercy."

"Will we make it?"

"I think so. It'll be close."

The relief came first, icy cold. Then the anger. "No more inexplicable numbnesses?" I asked.

"No. Why?"

"If any come up you'll be sure and tell me, won't you?"

"Are you getting at something?"

"Skip it." I wasn't angry any more.

"I'll be damned if I do. You know perfectly well it was mechanical trouble. You fixed it yourself!"

ALL THE MYRIAD WAYS

"No. I convinced you I must have fixed it. You needed to believe the rams *should* be working again. I gave you a miracle cure, Eric. I just hope I don't have to keep dreaming up new placebos for you all the way home."

"You thought that, but you went out on the wing sixteen miles up?" Eric's machinery snorted. "You've got guts where you need brains, Shorty."

I didn't answer.

"Five thousand says the trouble was mechanical. We let the mechanics decide after we land."

"You're on."

"Here comes the rocket. Two, one—"

It came, pushing me down into my metal suit. Sooty flames licked past my ears, writing black on the green metal ceiling, but the rosy mist before my eyes was not fire.

The man with the thick glasses spread a diagram of the Venus ship and jabbed a stubby finger at the trailing edge of the wing. "Right around here," he said. "The pressure from outside compressed the wiring channel a little, just enough so there was no room for the wire to bend. It had to act as if it were rigid, see? Then when the heat expanded the metal these contacts pushed past each other."

"I suppose it's the same design on both wings?"

He gave me a queer look. "Well, naturally."

I left my check for $5000 in a pile of Eric's mail and hopped a plane for Brasilia. How he found me I'll never know, but the telegram arrived this morning.

HOWIE COME HOME ALL IS FORGIVEN
                    DONOVANS BRAIN

I guess I'll have to.